BETWEEN IRAQ & HARD PLACES

THE JOURNEY OF A KURDISH ARTIST

ZUHDI SARDAR

GlobalEdAdvance
Press

Between Iraq & Hard Places
Copyright © 2011 by Zuhdi A. Sardar

Library of Congress Control Number: 2011938653
Sardar, Zuhdi A. - 1938
Between Iraq & Hard Places
ISBN 978-1-935434-08-5

Subject Codes and Description:
    1. DRA015000: Drama: Middle Eastern 2. FIC014000: Fiction-Historical-General 3.HIS027010: History: Military-Biological and Chemical Warfare

Cover design by Darrin Hoover
Cover art by Zuhdi Sardar

        Printed in the United States of America
All rights reserved, including the right to reproduce this book or any part thereof in any form, except for inclusion of written permission of the author and GlobalEdAdvancePRESS.

The Press does not have ownership of the contents of a book; this is the author's work and the author owns the copyright. All theory, concepts, constructs, and perspectives are those of the author and not necessarily the Press. They are presented for open and free discussion of the issues involved. All comments and feedback should be directed to the Email: *comments4author@aol.com* and they will be forwarded to the author for response.

        Published by
        FACT•ION
     -fiction based on fact-

        an imprint of
    GlobalEd Advance Press
       gea-books.com

Dedication

I dedicate this book to the thousands of innocent victims who suffered as a result of the Iraqi military attack on my hometown during the summer of 1963.

That evening ten of my best friends were sitting among a number of students and teachers, enjoying the Spring weather, playing dominoes in a local, open-air teahouse. But, in an instant, they were gone; the unwitting victims of Saddam Hussein's Baath regime attacks from Barzan to Halabja.

This book is in remembrance of all the hundreds of thousands of innocent Kurdish men, women and children who died as a result of biochemical attacks and were buried in mass unmarked graves throughout my homeland. This was the result of Saddam's Arabization.

...Let us never forget.

The Well

In a lush valley, just east of Halabja, green blades of grass swayed in the breeze. The pasture's beauty was framed by a clear sky and a background of plum-colored mountains, as old as time.

Into this scene three horses danced, nipping at each other, playfully anticipating the chase. The dominant of the trio, a stallion, the shade of iron-drenched soil, paused, and with his white mane tossing in the wind, he turned towards a nearby stream and set off in a gallop. Seeing this, his two companions, both angel white, followed; nipping and neighing at one another.

Delan watched the horses from his vantage point just behind the stone wall that completed the picture. Though entertained, he was surprised at how rough the trio played and wondered why he felt such a curious edge of tension in this usually tranquil place.

Gazing back at his easel, where the beauty of the valley and the galloping trio were being captured on canvas, he flicked his brush with a practiced flair; growing grass and contrasting violets with each stroke. The peaceful surroundings were Delan's refuge, his place of escape; a private sanctuary where he could paint and pick narcissus to his heart's content.

As he inhaled a freshly picked cluster of the flowers laying at his feet, its scent of Spring was an aromatic reminder that in a few days it would be Newroz, the Kurdish New Year, the day of the first liberation. With that reminder, he flashed on the duties that awaited him at home. And with a sigh of responsibility, he put down his brush and packed up his easel, paints and canvas.

As he turned for his walk back to the village, part of Delan longed to stay. This picturesque place was his refuge, his painter's paradise; his escape from the dangers that lay just beyond the plum-colored mountains, from the threats that put everyone he knew in harms way.

Reaching the walls of his village, old and marked by generations of triumphs and defeats, he passed the main street's teahouse, crowded with people he'd known all his life.

"Delan!" a familiar voice called to him from inside.

Turning, with easel and canvas in tow, he spotted his older brother Danna, and friend Saman, waving from a table cluttered with dominos.

"Can we see?" Danna gestured to the cloth-covered canvas.

"It's not ready," the painter shrugged his shoulders, clutching his creation close.

All the men at the surrounding tables stopped their games, and a hush came over the teahouse.

Realizing there was no getting out of it, Delan hesitantly raised the cloth. A collective sigh wafted through the open-air establishment.

"So you finally painted that red horse," Danna nodded, his broad youthful smile concealing the truth of his 30 years. "Beautiful." Turning to the men around him, he beamed, "Not so bad for my little brother."

"I've seen that horse," Saman acknowledged, slapping the table, causing his line of dominoes to jump. "Nice work."

"Thank you," Delan bowed slightly as he hurriedly re-covered the painting. "I'd better get going."

"No, stay! Play!," Danna gestured to the game.

"I can't –and neither should you. The well... Remember the well? We have to finish it."

"That won't take long," the older sibling glanced around at his friends. "Yesterday we hit wet soil."

"Danna," Delan glared with a familiar stare of exasperation. "Come on. Mom wants it done."

Tearing Danna away from his friends was never easy. Even on the way home, as they passed the bazaar Danna, the out-going brother, stopped to greet friends and chat with neighbors. While Delan, burdened with the ever-increasing weight of his painting supplies, urged his elder with constant reminders of "Mom".

The brothers were as different as night and day. Danna was flamboyant, the ever-energetic social sibling, while handsome Delan was broodish, artistically moody and quiet. Sometimes Delan envied his older brother's many friends. And Danna often wished he was as focused and diligent as Delan. But what they shared was a common physical bond to tend to their family land, as well as an equal love and respect for their mother.

"The Well!," their mother called out from the balcony, as the two passed through the gate. "Get back to work!," she pointed to the gaping hole in their yard. "Maybe today you'll get down to water."

Looking deep into the dark vertical shaft at his feet, Delan called out wearily, "Just need to put my paints away."

Working on the well was a difficult chore. When finished it would be a valuable, indispensable asset to the family; their very own convenient source of unlimited water.

Turning up the stone pathway, lined with bright, colorful bursts of flowers, Delan could smell the sweetness of his mother's bread baking. And walking quickly through the kitchen, determined to finish the well without distraction, he entered his room, and wearily set down his canvas amid his clutter of drawings, paints and brushes.

Setting up his easel he carefully placed his newest effort in the center of the room. And gazing once more at the oil rendering of the horses he was reminded again of how uncharacteristically rough they had played.

Outside, Delan made his way through the garden to the jagged threshold of the well. From there he could see his mother in the kitchen window, nodding her approval. Over his shoulder, not far from the well, he saw Danna resting on the ground pulling weeds.

"I'll be there ," he waved.

***

Delan descended into the well slowly, using the deep groves cut in the wall as a ladder. Reaching the bottom, he glancing up and signaled to Danna, now peering over the side, to lower the tools.

Moving mud was much harder than digging dry soil, and in no time Delan's back was in knots. After ten minutes of grunting stabs at the dirt, he paused and wrenched himself upright, for a stretch. But in that moment of relief, his ears caught the unmistakable flutter of birds above. Looking up, he glimpsed their white wings pass over the jagged opening.

Something had disturbed them.

Before he could think there was another flutter. This one, below him; a deep, booming rumble. As it reverberated under his feet, his mind flashed on the strange behavior of the horses. And the horrible rumble grew louder.

The earth began to shake. Then, came a strange sudden lull, as if the earth paused to gather its strength.

"Delan!," his brother called from above.

An instant later the full force of earth's grinding returned; shaking the well walls, loosening more mud and rock than his shovel could ever achieve. Delan tried to protect his head from the debris, grabbing for roots, rocks - anything that would keep him upright.

Desperately he spun in place, searching the well's depths for refuge. That's when he saw it- a great surge of mud and water swirling, swelling up from the floor of the shaft.

The ground beneath him gave way. And though he managed to clutch a nearby outcropping of roots, it slipped through his fingers. And Delan felt himself drop into the unknown.

Suddenly submerged in the cold, murky water, he struggled to find the surface. The need for air pushed his racing heart. Finally, spitting mud, his head broke through, only to be met by a rain of rocks.

Reaching up to pull himself against the wall for protection, Delan's right shoulder exploded in pain as a large rock struck him. The impact instantly stopped his forward momentum and forced him once more to sink under the well's icy swirl.

Kicking his way back to the air, his leg scraped a jagged shard of wood, sending a searing jolt through his calf. As his mind fought to think of anything but the pain, Delan realized that, somewhere during his struggle, the earth had stopped shaking.

The world had gone silent.

Cold, wet and in agony, he knew that he was trapped, alone. And surmising that he had no other choice but to move, Delan picked a direction, and pushed himself forward.

Slowly, he felt his way through the pitch black. The icy water, up about his chin. Each foot forward seemed to take forever. Each breath burned. Yet he pressed on, certain that if he stopped, or even slowed down, the claustrophobic shaft surrounding him would become his grave.

Just as that thought took hold, Delan saw a speck of light in the distance. Picking up the pace, he stumbled forward ever faster.

Wading through the muddy water Delan begged God to save him, even thought a part of him knew that this was how people died – drawn to the light. Still, he pushed his aching body, moving both earth and water to reach the small opening.

The canopy of sky just above him was the top of a well. Not his, but his neighbor's! Realizing this, he inhaled a stabbing breath and yelled for help.

Nothing.

Forcing his water-frozen legs to climb, he pushed his exhausted frame up the well's wall, clawing his way to back to the world.

Eventually feeling a breeze through the opening, weary Delan called out, again. "Help! ...Somebody!"

Nothing, but the wind.

Spotting a rope dangling through the well's opening, he grabbed for it. Feeling too weak to climb out, he tied the cord about his chest to support his aching legs, and called out once more.

No one.

As his hopes and strength faded so did his vision, and drifting into unconsciousness, his head slumped, hovering mere inches above the water.

***

When Delan came to, the sun was directly above him. Once again he took a sharp, painful breath and called for help. Still there was no answer.

The numbness in his legs had lessened the pain, so he lifted himself out of the water until his back was against the mud wall. Raising his good leg he pushed his foot against the other side and slowly pulled himself up with the rope.

Straining, he managed to lift his head above the stone mouth of the well. The sunlight was painful, but he squinted towards the neighbors' house. Strangely, it was completely intact. It made no sense. There wasn't even a crack.

Painfully, Delan closed his eyes and pulled his body over the top of the well. Never in his life had he felt such relief. But when he opened his eyes, all happiness drained from him; for he was starring into the face of the neighbor's little boy, laying a few feet away. Blood dripped from his mouth and nose. His eyes were open, yet unseeing.

Raising himself Delan saw another body on the other side of the child; the boy's mother. Her arms lay outstretched, as if reaching for her child.

Though weak, Delan could not keep himself from crying. Frantically he tried to feel for heartbeats, praying they were somehow, miraculously, alive. But there was nothing but the distant stare of eyes turned to the heavens, as if asking *why*.

Delan closed his own, and sobbed.

He had no idea how this had happened, how an earthquake had done this to these people, but knew he had to find his own family. It's just these two, he told himself. Everyone else is fine.

Beads of sweat dripped into his eyes as his struggled to drag himself to a nearby woodpile. When he got there his breathing was ragged, tears mixed with sweat on his face. "Can't rest," he thought, "I don't have time." Finding a long sturdy piece of wood, he used it to support his weight and eventually stand.

Hobbling to the gate with his crutch, he realized the whole world was unnervingly silent. He quickened his pace, fear now giving him a burst of adrenaline. But when he reached the edge of the yard he froze. Before him, the street was littered with people, hunched over, holding each other. Transfixed, Delan realized that no one was moving.

He had to get to his house. Everywhere he turned there was death. A man, mouth open, slumped over the steering wheel of his car. A mother and daughter, leaning against the side of their house, arms wrapped around each other in a final embrace. A little girl, laying in the street as if she'd stumbled from the sidewalk, her dog beside her. And scattered among the bodies were birds of every kind.

It had to be a nightmare. None of this could be happening. The silence. The death.

When Delan reached his house, the front door was open. Immediately he knew his family had not been spared. There, in the threshold, was his father, holding his little brother, Serwan, as if trying to protect him with his own body. The only sound now was Delan's racking sobs.

Gently he turned his father over and, for the last time, looked into his eyes before closing them. Beside him was Serwan, his little brother, the one who'd kept his family laughing with mischievous antics, now motionless.

Delan started shaking, unable to comprehend what was happening. Slowly he rose, leaning heavily on his wood crutch.

His mother. He needed to find his mother. She would be fine, he knew. As he walked inside the house he looked for her, expecting to find her in the kitchen, perhaps, huddled in a corner and crying, but alive. Together they would comfort each other. He'd bury his head in her shoulder and never, never, would leave her side again.

Yet there she lay. Her body crumpled on the kitchen floor, her face hidden under her thick dark hair.

He couldn't look. He couldn't think.

Suddenly his brother's face flashed across his mind, and he raced out the back door. Hobbling to the side of the house, he prayed with each painful step that somehow Danna was spared. But when he saw the figures of four young men on the ground near the gate, his steps slowed. As he drew closer, he saw his brother, staring up at the sky, his brown eyes fixed, twigs caught in his hair. A small trickle of blood rested beneath his nose.

Wordlessly he sank to his knees and wrapped his arms around his dead brother. Then laying down next to him, Delan nestled himself between his brother and his three childhood friends. Turning, he studied his brother's profile, the tears streaming silently down his face.

***

When the nurse from the Red Cross found him, Delan was clutching his brother's arm and talking to him through tears. It took two more Red Cross aids to separate him from Danna, and when they loaded him into a truck with other survivors, the young painter stared out the window vacantly and called for his mother, his father and brothers.

"They're all dead," a man seated across from him, muttered. "All of them. Thousands of them."

"Do you know his name?," the nurse gestured to her discovery.

"Delan."

On the driver's shortwave radio, an emergency broadcast cut into the silence. "..Survivors are presently being rescued and taken to Iran... Again, the Iraqis bombed the town of Halabja just hours ago. It appears that nerve gas and mustard gas were used, though the motive is unclear. The Red Cross is placing the estimate of those killed at roughly five thousand. Again, five thousand innocent men, women and children have been killed in the town of Halabja."

Paris

Though many of the survivors were sent to Tehran, Senendag and Mahabad, Iran. Delan, along with a few others, were sent to France to be examined, in hopes that the nature of the bombing could be better understood. For hours the doctors studied the tissue of his burned skin, while the nurses did their best to get Delan to talk. But with his arm and leg in a cast, he stared blankly at the ceiling and said nothing.

"Delan," Nurse Matilde entered his room smiling. "You have visitors, some of your countrymen. Maybe you can talk to them." Turning to the two men who had followed her in, she raised her eyebrows. "Good luck. He doesn't talk to anyone."

Simko, the shorter of the two men, approached Delan's bed and introduced himself in Kurdish. After a silent moment, the man continued. "I'm sorry about the bombing. I understand it must be painful to talk about, but it would help us if you could tell us what happened, and how it happened."

The two men waited for a response. But when none came, the taller of the two turned to the nurse.

"Maybe he lost his hearing?"

"No. He can hear fine, he just doesn't answer. He saw a lot, it takes its toll."

The tall man leaned in closer to Delan and whispered something in Kurdish. Still, there was no trace of expression on his face. "He can't hear," the man said, under his breath.

At this, Nurse Matilde dropped the glass she was carrying. The sound of shattering glass filled the room, and every head turned, including Delan's. Then, just like that, Delan was back to staring at the ceiling.

"In a couple of weeks we'll take his casts off," she smiled. "If there's no improvement in his mental state, we might have to send him to an institution better equipped for his needs."

"Would it be okay if we came in, once a week maybe?" Simko suggested, "You know, talk to him; see if he responds."

"That would be nice. I just hope he recovers. He looks like such a nice young man. This shouldn't' have happened to him. Or anyone, of course."

"Here's our number," the tall man offered, handing her his card, "In case there's any change."

But the next day there was no change. And when they returned a week later, Delan was still staring silently at the ceiling.

As they turned to leave, Matilde offered, "Delan had two Iraqi visitors. You just missed them."

Simko stopped midstep and turned, "Who were they?"

Pulling a business card from her pocket she glanced at the printed words, "They said they were from the Iraqi Human Rights Organization.

Taking the card Simko exchanged glances with his partner. "There is no such an organization in Iraq. This is a front for Saddam's secret agency."

Matilde's eyes widened, stunned.

"Do you mind if I keep this card?"

"Go ahead."

As the two men turned, the frightened nurse added, "Delan is scheduled to be moved to another facility next week."

"The name?"

"St. Anne's Mental Hospital."

***

Twelve months later, Delan was in a chair by the window, hands folded in his lap.

"Whoever works with him, needs to be patient." Dr. Beegee advised his four nurses. "It's been over a year since he's spoken."

The psychiatrist paused, gazed at his patient with empathy, then continued. "Friends, family, everyone he knew – was killed in the poison gas bombing. Imagine what that would do to a person."

The women exchanged nervous glances.

Then Severeen, a brunette with vibrant blue eyes, stepped forward. Stooping next to Delan's chair, she carefully studied everything; the small scars on his hands, the blank expression in his eyes.

"Though only about twenty-five years old," the doctor had continued, "this man looks as though he's been through a lifetime of suffering."

"Severeen, " Dr. Beegee questioned, "are you willing to work with him?"

Quickly rising, the young nurse realized she should not have stepped forward to get a better look. Now the doctor was gazing at her with hope in his eyes. Averting her eyes, she stole a quick glance back at Delan's emotionless face.

"Of course, this patient represents a bit of a challenge," the doctor acknowledged. "But I'm sure that would be a valuable experience for you both. Am I right?"

Severeen stood silent, not knowing what to say.

"Any progress, no matter how small, will be a great reward."

Placing her hand on the back of Delan's chair, she offered the psychiatrist a hesitant smile. "Alright. I'll give it a shot."

The next day, Delan was sitting in the Activity Room, staring at a painting on the wall, when an old man wheeled himself beside him. For a few minutes the gentleman sat silent, waiting for some sort of acknowledgement or greeting. But when none came he seemed determined to plow forward.

"How come you're so quiet? Didn't they feed you breakfast this morning? No visitors, is that it? That would get anyone down, I know." When the old man stopped to take a breath, he realized that Delan offered no response, but with nothing better to do, he continued.

"Maybe you just prefer not to talk? Who was that, in that short story, who answered everything with *I'd prefer not to*? Eh. You don't know. Well, that's fine by me. I'll do all the talking, for you and for me. My daughter says I talk too much, maybe that's why I'm here."

Delan looked out towards the window. The old man grunted. "Well, quiet people are one thing, rude another."

Severeen, standing on the other side of the room, watched the old man leave. Now it was her turn.

As she approached, she could see Delan registering another person in the flicker of his eyes, yet still he faced the window.

"I'm Severeen," she said, as she brought a chair beside him. She held both his hands in hers and yet even with the human contact there was no sign of recognition.

"Delan, I'm here to help you recover, but I need your cooperation." She looked down, at his slippered feet. "I know you've experienced pain. And I can't even begin to understand what you've been through, but I want to help. I can help. But you have to let me."

Still he looked out the window towards a tree with pale, shimmering green leaves. His hands were limp in her grasp. Across the room, a woman began to scream someone's name, over and over.

"How about a walk," Severeen suggested, standing, holding out her hand. "Let's get out of this place. Would you like that?"

Gently she pulled him up, and without looking in her eyes, he did as she asked.

Outside was a small courtyard, a path of stones that laced through bright flowers. Severeen led Delan through them like a blind man. When they stood before a bench, she sat and gently pulled him towards her. Slowly he took a seat, and Severeen massaged his hand, looking for any sign of feeling. Still he remained unchanged, staring at a dead bird next to a pot of azaleas. She lifted his hand to her mouth and bit his finger. Nothing.

Reluctantly she lowered his hand, and likewise studied the dead bird, wondering what to do.

The next day, Severeen found Delan at his place alongside the window, facing a fellow patient with a large pad of drawing paper. The man drew lines, then tore the page off and stuck it in a pile. Over and over.

She studied Delan's eyes, which didn't move, and yet he seemed to be watching the man. He hadn't turned away. Taking note of what the man was drawing, she watched him form a big circle on the page. Then put two circles inside, like eyes. The mouth, when he added it, was outside the circle.

Severeen smiled and looked back at Delan, who was still looking at the paper; now there was a slight lift to his mouth. Severeen's heart began to race. Was that the start of a smile? She turned to the patient. "Can I have this?"

The patient handed it over without a glance, and Severeen held the drawing closer to Delan's face. His expression, however, did not change. Maybe she'd been imagining things. Still, exposure was key. Books, paintings, animals, whatever he needed to stimulate his mind. She lowered the drawing and looked into his eyes.

Somehow she would figure it out.

***

Severeen kept her apartment at a low temperature, both for the sake of the cost of utilities, as well as for the coziness that blankets, sweaters, mugs of steaming tea induced. The apartment was on the left bank and was filled with plants, vases and baskets of dried flowers. Finding old furniture and reinventing it was what she loved – a chaise reupholstered, a nightstand painted in a soft yellow, a table with bright enamel drawer pulls. Shabby chic, she supposed, was the term for her place, but to Severeen it was just romantic. Lace curtains, silver candleholders. Even the paintings, all done in pastels, spoke of love and longing.

Her apartment was her escape. Once she walked through the door and closed it behind her, she shed the day like a coat. Then curling up in a chair with an open book to read, she would slip away for a much-needed rest from her patients.

But Delan was different. He was the challenge that would not let her go. Even when she closed the door behind her, the wheels of Severeen's mind kept turning. When she curled up in her chair, her book would remained untouched, as her mind wondered about what sounds, fabrics, what cultural stimulation would unlock Delan from his prison.

Her patient was becoming such an obsession, that the young nurse almost did not notice when the doorbell rang, for the third time.

"Severeen! Hey, let us in – it's Paul and Chantal."

When she let her friends in, they immediately made themselves at home on the couch.

"So," Paul grinned, accepting a glass of Severeen's wine, 'at last we have verification that they did not lock you up at the hospital with your patients,"

"I know. I've been a bad friend."

"It's okay. You're forgiven," Chantal raised her glass, as if toasting. "See how easy we are?"

"I wish everyone was."

Paul took the bottle from her and looked at the label. "Where's that Domaine Des Ravanes cabernet?"

Severeen smiled. "Still being saved."

"One day you'll see that the best occasion is just this," he gestured to all present, including himself.

"I know. I know. I actually came close to opening it last week. Bad day at work, all I wanted was to drown my troubles."

"I take it that curing the mentally unstable isn't going so well,"Chantal leaned forward.

"It's fine. It's just this one patient - the one I'm working with, of course. I knew going in that it wouldn't be easy – Dr. Beegee all but said it was hopeless. So I don't know. I'm being hard on myself. He is in a state of shock and I can't figure out how to reach him. He's in there," she pointed to her own head, "I know he is. I just can't get to him."

"That's just like you," Paul chucked. "Pick the one guy who wants nothing to do with you."

Severeen laughed. "I know. It was his eyes. They're deep, rich brown and kind. But there's also such sadness in them. It's almost painful."

"What's his story?" Chantal fished, glancing at Paul with a playful glint.

"He's a Kurd. Was in Halabja when the government bombed them. He basically saw his entire family and just about everyone he ever knew die."

Paul's grin faded. "That would put some sadness in my eyes too. Jesus. How the hell do you help someone like that?"

"I don't know. That's the problem. I'm thinking I need to learn more about his culture, so I can find a way to relate to him; to show he recognizes something that might jerk him back the present. All I really know about the Kurds is that they number about twenty-four million and have no country. That and they've been betrayed by just about everyone. Other than that..."

"They have a.... a cultural center," Paul recalled, snapping his fingers repeatedly. "The Kurdish Institute of Paris. You should go there. I have a friend who has a friend, who worked there. The guy was Kurdish. I met him a few times, great guy. Anyhow, I think they have a library."

"Maybe they'd have a way of finding someone who knows Delan!" Severeen scooted to the edge of her chair.

Paul laughed. "Yeah, twenty-four million people...I'm sure they all know each other."

When Chantal and Paul left, Severeen swallowed the last of her wine, and stared at the wall for a moment. Then, setting down her glass she looked up the Kurdish Institute's number immediately and picked up the phone.

After detailing the situation, explaining that finding someone – anyone – recognizable would help enormously in Delan's recovery, Severeen was assured that someone would call her back.

But as she hung up the phone, her enthusiasm melted. Remembering Paul's words, she thought about the odds. The entire population of Delan's village was basically murdered. Who would be left? Who would stay?

Three days later, the phone rang. Severeen, in the midst of doing dishes, grabbed a towel and raced to the phone.

"I am Dr. Rahman, from the Kurdish Center. I understand you're inquiring about Delan Marif. He's a relative of mine. I know his family well."

Severeen tried to remain calm. "I believe I – eh, from what I understand, his parents were killed. Is that correct?"

"Yes. Along with two brothers."

"I'm sorry for your loss. Losing an entire family. I can't imagine."

"Thank you. But it was not the whole family. Delan has another brother in Sweden, and a sister in Sulaymaniyah, Kurdistan. She's married to a teacher there.""

Severeen's mind was racing. This was better than she could have hoped – two immediate family members. "Do you know how I can get in touch with them?"

"His brother left Sweden for Halabja, but I'm not sure if he stayed. We'll try and get in touch with his sister. She might be easier to reach. By the way, do you think it would be alright if I took Delan to dinner next week?"

"I'd have to ask the hospital and get back to you, but I don't see why not."

When she hung up, she immediately called Paul. "Wow. You know Dr. Rahman?"

"He's a relative of Delan's. Why?"

"No. I mean, besides being a relative – he's a local Kurdish leader. I remember, that guy - the Kurd I knew - was trying to find a way to meet with Rahman. He's a hard one to get to. I hear the Iraqi Secret Service watches his every move. The man goes nowhere without a bodyguard."

Severeen was silent, suddenly nervous. Maybe she was in over her head. But what could she do now?

***

Dr. Beegee was elated that a relative of Delan's was discovered, and a respected one at that. "Of course he can take him to dinner! Though you might want to warn Dr. Rahman that in Delan's current state he might not be the best conversationalist."

Severeen agreed, and called the doctor at the Kurdish Center the minute she got home. As she waited for him to answer, she rifled through her mail, pausing when she saw a card from her mother. She'd completely forgotten – her mother's birthday the week before. Here Delan would do anything to see his own mother, while Severeen completely forgot and ignored her own.

"Severeen?"

"Yes, Dr. Rahman. Good news. You can take Delan to dinner. Just ask for me when you arrive at the hospital."

"Wonderful! Thank you. This means a lot."

The evening of the dinner, Severeen watched from the window as a car pulled into the lot of their hospital wing. Sure enough, two dark haired men, one a bodyguard-type, got out, checked the address and entered. She turned from the window, just as a white car pulled up to the doctor's car and paused, before parking a few spaces over.

Immediately Severeen liked Dr. Rahman; a small man with white hair at his temples and a kind, weathered face. He greeted Delan warmly, and Severeen felt the first real hope when Delan looked up at his relative with silent recognition.

Dr. Rahman looked disappointed, but hopeful.

"It's alright. He recognizes me. It's a start."

Severeen smiled encouragingly. "Back by eight o'clock please. And I bet he'll be talking."

At the window, she watched Dr. Rahman carefully hold onto Delan's arm, leading him to the car. Everything appeared fine. But for some reason the young nurse couldn't help feel a twinge of anxiety.

As Rahman opened the car door, Delan didn't move. A sudden fear swirled in his eyes. Realizing this must be his first time in a public arena in over a year, Rahman took the younger man's hand and whispered a reassuring, "Everything is all right."

After a few minutes of gentle prodding Delan relaxed enough and stepped out onto the sidewalk. The bodyguard waited till the two were safely inside the restaurant, then drove a couple of blocks up the street to an empty parking spot.

Dr. Rahman and Delan had already taken a table at the far end of the restaurant, up against the wall, when the bodyguard entered. "Go," Rahman waved him towards the bar, "Have some tea, order something."

Scanning the layout, the guard noted that from the bar he could sit casually, out of the way, but with clear unobstructed view of the crowded room.

"This place is packed," Rahman added, 'Only a fool would try anything here. Go."

The bottle of wine the waiter brought was displayed for Dr. Rahman's approval, the cork set beside him. He nodded, and the waiter filled both their glasses. Delan stared at the red liquid, held in candlelight, dark as blood.

"Delan," Dr. Rahman's voice was warm, inviting. "Look at me."

Patiently the doctor waited till Delan's eyes shifted, and peered into his. Then moving his wine glass aside, he leaned across the table, never breaking their mutual gaze. "There is hope for you." he smiled, patting Delan's hand. "Come back to us, to our world. You are a gifted artist. We need you."

At the mention of his art, Delan looked up slightly and to the left, as if remembering.

***

An hour later, as they were about to exit the restaurant, the bodyguard reappeared. Stepping between the two men and the door, he held up his hand. "Please, wait here. I'll bring the car around,"

Putting the doctor's car in reverse, the vehicle's tires rolled only one revolution when the back end abruptly rose then fell with a jarring bang. Immediately the driver slammed on the brakes, threw open the door and found that both back tires had simultaneously blown. And getting out for a closer look, he saw the spike strip.

Waiting in the restaurant foyer, the doctor glanced at his watch. "He said he parked two blocks away from here. He must be turning around," Taking Delan arm, Rahman opened the door. "We'll meet him halfway. After a meal like that, a little walk never hurt anyone."

Realizing that they had walked a half block without a word, the doctor attempted to break the silence. "Did you like your lamb? Nothing like the Kurds, of course, but the French know their way around a kitchen."

As he waited for Delan's reply, they approached the corner of a dimly lit street, Anticipating the dark, Rahman took hold of the younger man's arm. Doing so, the stride of the two men fell in unison. And for a moment the synchronized cadence of their steps created a sense of calm between them; a bond that needed no words.

But four steps later, their bliss was interrupted by the sudden appearance of three figures out the shadows. The next instant brought an explosion of flying fists, wrenching the two men apart. The attack was brief, but brutal. For a fleeting moment the half lit side street became a confusing blur of cracking bones, muted moans and curses. And at its crescendo Dr. Rahman's small, broken frame was thrown against a wall, held there by strong hands and gutted with a knife,

Seeing Rahman's body crumble to the pavement, Delan lunged for the knife-wielding figure, But the butt of a gun slammed against his temple and he likewise slumped the sidewalk with a breath-taking thud.

When he finally gathered the strength to open his eyes, Delan found himself once more on the ground, gazing at the lifeless body of another relative, just a few feet away.

Laying there, too weary and heartbroken to move, Delan studied Dr. Rahman's emotionless face and listened as the clatter of several feet ran erratically up the street. After a brief lull, there was a muffled echo of shouts and the fire-cracker pop of a pistol firing twice. Then, the hurried patter of a single pair of shoes approached.

Into his line of sight, the bodyguard's hard-soled shoes skidded to a stop. Breathing heavy, the man gazed down at the old doctor's broken body. And with a whimper of genuine remorse, he knelt and tore through the bloody clothes, in a frantic, futile search for life.

Eventually, the man sat back on his heels, spent. And in that silence, he heard Delan moan.

***

When Severeen arrived at the hospital, the lobby was filled with Kurds, low whispers and cries of grief.

Recognizing the bodyguard, she anxiously worked her way across the crowded room. But as he came into full view, so did the bloody stains on his shirt.

"Dr. Rahman?" she hesitantly asked.

The bodyguard closed his eyes and shook his head.

"Delan?"

"He's being examined. He said he was fine?

"He?...Who, which doctor?"

"Not the doctor. Delan."

A Well of Dreams

"Just a few doors...down the hall." Repeating the directions she was given, Severeen slowly walked through the hospital corridor in search of Delan.

After passing 'a few' empty rooms, a door opened just a few steps ahead.. As the doctor exited, Severeen glimpsed the patient inside. Picking up her pace, she passed the door and caught up with the doctor as he walked.

"Excuse me, I'm a nurse at Saint Anne's. The man you're treating, Delan, he's a patient of mine. How is he?"

"There were some harsh blows to the head." he offered, checking his clipboard. "But, all tests, so far, have come back normal. I'd like to keep him over night to be sure."

"May I see him?"

"He's pretty tired, He may not talk much."

Sprouting a smile, she stopped and started back the other direction. "It's alright, any talking is good,"

The doctor paused, his forehead furrowed. Then resumed his stride.

When she opened the door, her smile faded.

With his head bandaged and cheek bruised, Delan sat on the table staring vacantly out the window.

'He's gone back," she thought. "He's not with us anymore. The trauma was too much."

Lightly, so as not to frighten him, she touched his hand. He turned, as if not understanding, then gazing up into Severeen's eyes – there it was, recognition.

"Delan, I'm so glad you're alright!"

Still he said nothing, just stared at her. She let go of his hand, and went to a table against the wall where she saw his chart laying beside a jar of cotton balls.

"Do I know you?"

Never in her life had she been so happy to answer a question. "You do. Yes. I'm Severeen, I work at the," she paused, trying to decide what to tell right now. Clearly his short-term memory was compromised. She turned from the table and saw the doctor in the doorway, watching. "We can talk about it tomorrow. You need your rest."

Delan just nodded, then turned again towards the window.

Back in the lobby, Severeen found the bodyguard slumped in a chair. "So sorry about Dr. Rahman. The loss - it's beyond words."

He looked up at her, his eyes red, his big face filled with guilt and sorrow. "I was looking for a grey car," he said. "They were in a grey car."

"Who are *they*?

"Saddam's men. Anyone who's important to us, to our cause, they kill." He looked down at the aged linoleum floor. "I thought they were in a grey car. I thought it was safe."

"They knew that," Severeen said. "They planned it that way. There was nothing you could do. Please, if you need any help, let me know."

The bodyguard nodded, then stopped, his head still bowed.

***

The next day, Severeen walked slowly down the hallway towards Delan's room. If he didn't remember her, there was a good chance he also didn't remember the events that led to his state of shock. Telling him that his family had been killed was not something she was looking forward to.

When she walked in, again there was recognition in his eyes.

"I'm Severeen. The intern assigned to assist with your rehabilitation."

He nodded.

"I'm here to help you regain your conscious mind. You've been in a state of shock. They brought you here from your country, over a year ago, to study your skin. The burns."

Delan looked down, as if gathering his thoughts.

Slowly, Severeen continued, hoping and dreading that she might jog his memory. "Your hometown,

Halabja, was bombed, with three different types of poison gas."

His eyes shut tight, as if to hold back the sudden flood of images. His breathing quickened, labored, then shallowed to final deep breath. When he opened his wet eyes, their distance glaze was gone.

He was emerging from his dark well of dreams.

"The horses... they knew what was coming. It was home... paradise... I kept forgetting, I should remember more, but it... slips away." Pausing his eyes brightened. "It was Saddam's men?"

"Yes."

"But... you said I was brought here more than a year ago. Just yesterday I saw one of my relatives?"

"Yes, that was here in Paris. Dr. Rahman."

"Dr. Rahman? Was here?"

"He came to visit you. Actually many Kurds did. He took you out to dinner, do you remember? Do you remember what happened ...after?"

Delan looked straight at her, and she knew it had come back to him. "Why?" he whispered, though it was not a question. "Saddam's men again. No one will leave us alone – All we want is peace. Even far away, they find us."

He shook his head, angrily.

"Nixon, Kissinger, Reagan, Bush. England and Russia. Always we've been betrayed; always we've had to fight for our homeland, just to exist. That's all we want, just to exist. But how can twenty-five million exist without a country, when the rest of the world fights to keep them down? To keep power from their hands? It's greed – why can't they leave us be. We only defend ourselves. Still they come back, wanting the oil. All we want is the land where we were born."

Severeen could say nothing. What does one say when one's identity is always being challenged? Everything in her life she took for granted: Her language, her songs, her safety.

Delan looked back out the window and took a deep breath. "What of Dr. Rahman's body?"

"They're flying it to Sulaymaniyah."

"He came to visit me and was killed."

"It wasn't your fault. Besides, you were almost killed. Not just once, but twice. You'll be released from here tomorrow. Given your regained consciousness, you won't be require to return to the institution. Maybe for a few tests, but that's it."

Delan nodded, gratefully.

"So the next issue is… where will you go?"

"I don't know anyone here."

"That's what I thought. I just had to be sure. Don't worry, I will help…you're not alone. So just concentrate on feeling better and I'll take care of the rest, okay?"

When Severeen left, she went straight to the institution to talk to Dr. Beegee.

"He can't stay here."

"I know doctor, and he wouldn't want to. Delan's better. This place would only hinder his further improvement."

"What are your ideas? Most families make arrangements upon release. Clearly going home isn't an option."

"A Kurdish refugee center?"

Dr. Beegee smiled. "It's a good idea, in theory, but after what happened they're flooded. What I'll do is send a report to the Ministry of Foreign Affairs, requesting political asylum on his behalf. His conditioned has improved, his life has been put in danger twice by his own government, so I would think – no, I would pray hat the request would be granted. But there will be an interim period. These things take time."

***

The next day Severeen returned to the hospital. "Check back with me before he's released," Dr. Beegee reminded her. "We'll see if anything's developed. Surely we can get at least one organization to release some funds."

Severeen looked at her watch. It was only 10 am Anything could happen.

***

This time, Delan not only recognized her, but seemed happy to see her. She took a seat in an orange chair beside his bed. "No news yet," she said.

"I had a feeling."

"Delan, what do you do? What kind of work?"

"It's difficult to put my work into one category."

He smiled when he saw Severeen's confused, and perhaps alarmed, expression.

"I'm an artist. I like Expressionism, but when I do work from real life I tend to be more realistic." He laughed. "I guess that would make sense. I used to love impressionism. I paint landscapes and portraits. Lately I've used bolder colors and brush-strokes. I love the unexpected techniques that emerge in the process. I like to experiment with my art."

Without warning, his expression changed. "I just remembered my last canvas. I painted it just a few hours...before..."

" ...The bombing," Severeen sighed. "I'm sorry that something you love as much as painting is linked with that."

. "It was beautiful." Delan nodded. " Three horses in a field, near my hometown. They were playing rough, as if they were mad at each other. My brother and friends, they all liked it," he recalled with a hesitant smile. "At least they said they did... An Aspeshea is a special horse, one the Kurds find most beautiful. It's a light reddish brown color, with a white mane and tail." He looked out the window. "I loved painting."

"There's no reason you can't paint again. Maybe you can get a studio."

Delan formed a sad smile, as if he knew there was little hope, But appreciated the young nurse's effort to cheer him.

***

"I don't have good news, Severeen," Dr. Beegee shrugged. "I wish I did, but it's just too soon. As wonderful as his recovery is, it didn't give us much time to prepare."

"So what do we do? We can't send him back to the institution, that would be a setback."

"Without other options, I don't know." The doctor looked into Severeen's eyes. "What about you?"

"Me?"

"You could take him, he knows you. He trusts you."

"Am I allowed to?"

"Special circumstances, Severeen. Besides, it might only be a week, two weeks. Just till we get things in order. We'll have him stay one more night at the institute, check him out, and release him tomorrow. You'll have a night to yourself," He laughed." to tidy up a bit."

Severeen pictured her small apartment. As cramped as it would be, it was infinitely better than him staying at the institution.

"Talk to him," the doctor said. "Mention it to him and see what he says."

When Severeen opened Delan's door, he looked at her expectantly. Seeing the look on her face, he smiled. "You did what you could."

"Well, there is another option. So far the funds for your expenses haven't been released yet. But...would you like to stay with me? I mean, temporarily? You'd be back at the institution just for tonight, but after that?"

Delan studied her, as if waiting for a punch line.

"It's small, but like I said, it's temporary. It would be no problem."

"I wouldn't be an inconvenience?"

"Not if you don't mind the sofa-bed. It's a little rustic, but -" she stopped. She had no idea what his life was like. For all she knew, a sofa-bed in Kurdistan was a luxury.

Delan simply smiled, and thanked her for the offer.

***

"A night to myself," she thought. "The last night." The nurse had no idea what she was getting herself into – but it made sense. Out of the entire world, including distant relatives, *she* was the one he trusted. She glanced around the apartment, which was neat and only required a few minor adjustments: – put away tennis shoes, remove sweater from the back of a chair, store toiletries under the bathroom sink.

Once these few things were done, she flipped on the TV and started the dishes, listening to the news. That was the only thing, the dishes –No matter how clean she was, there always dishes in the sink. "Maybe that could be Delan's job," she pondered. "Free room and board in exchange for never having to wash the dishes,. Not a bad deal."

As she dunked her hands in the water to retrieve a wayward fork, she heard the newscaster say "Middle

East." Within seconds Severeen and her wet hands were standing, dripping, in front of the TV.

"...Iraqi President, Saddam Hussein, is accusing the West for the recent price reduction in oil; particularly singling out Kuwait for being the driving force behind OPEC's new policy."

"In related news, President Hussein has been maneuvering his military forces from the north to the south, close to the Kuwait border. Military analysts speculate this could mean Hussein has extravagant plans for the south, shifting his focus from the Kurds in the North..."

Just like that, the news changed to the weather.

Out of all the world's news, only one sentence made mention of the Kurds. But even Severeen, who professed little knowledge of Delan's people, recognized that all of the news was not being told.

New Beginning

"Take this," Dr. Beegee smiled, handing Severeen an envelop. "It's not much, but it should take care of a few basic needs. And, if necessary, my checkbook will help supplement the rest."

Reluctantly accepting the gift, Severeen sighed, "Doctor, you don't have to do this."

"A houseguest can be quite bothersome. And given Delan's unique situation, the last thing I want is for you to juggle a financial burden , too.."

"I'm sure the money will come through soon," she, replied, wistfully. "If not, I'll remember your offer."

"Alright then," the doctor nodded in the direction of Delan's room. "He is officially released into your care."

Delan, stood as the anxious young nurse entered, his duffel bag in his hand. He looked so lost, yet hopeful. "A little,orphaned boy, " she thought.

In the cab Delan sat with the duffel bag on his lap, his head turning at different landmarks, craning to see the tip of the Eiffel tower. "I always wanted to go to Paris, but not like this."

"No, I imagine not."

"Do you know anything about my brother? In Sweden?"

"Only that Dr. Rahman said he went to Sulaymaniyah after the bombing. He tried to contact him, but no luck."

"I am going to send my brother a letter to our home address. Maybe he will get it. Eventually I will also go back to see who survived. I hope I see him."

A little silence between them. Delan looks in the duffel bag. "I don't recognize any of the clothes in this bag."

Severeen smiled. "You weren't exactly yourself when you were wearing them. What did you wear at home? What kind of clothes?"

"Blue jeans, T-shirts. Normal clothes."

Severeen nodded, feeling foolish. Of course, the Middle East isn't all as seen on TV or in films.

"I guess I need clothes," he said, looking down at the bag in his lap. "There's a place a few streets from my apartment we'll go to. Second hand clothes, but it's nice. Nothing smells."

He laughed. "And do they give the clothing away, this place?"

"No, but it's a bargain, so it almost feels like it." She glanced at him. "I have some money for you, to help get you settled."

"Your money?"

Severeen could tell her guest would feel bad even if he knew it came from the doctor, so she shook her head. "It's just a bit before the rest comes in. Here," she said to the cab driver. "Right here's fine."

At the elevator, she remembered the food issue, but didn't want to insinuate he didn't eat "normal" food. "Tell me what kind of food you like."

"Anything that's not hospital food."

"That much I figured," she laughed.

"Back home, we cook a lot of vegetables in tomato sauce, with herbs and spices. Rice is always part of the meal. Stuffed eggplants, stuffed grape leaves and shish kebab."

"Wow. I gotta warn you, my pots and pans have never seen food like that. Do you cook those dishes?"

"Most of them. One night I'll cook for you."

She jiggled her keys, unlocked the door, and pushed it open. "Here we are."

He looked around the room. It was just like her. Exactly as he would have thought. "It looks like you."

"Randomly thrown together?"

"No. Relaxed. Feminine." She laughed. "Well, it's your turn to relax. There's the couch, your new home. The remote for the TV should be by that lamp." She tossed her keys and purse on the little kitchen table. "I'll throw something together for us to eat. But don't get your hopes up."

Delan flipped on the TV, and scanned the channels till he found the news. For a few minutes he tried watching, but the man's voice was annoying, whiney and nasal.

He looked to the table beside him. By the lamp was a picture, an image of Severeen and someone who looked rather similar to her, perhaps a sister. They were laughing, as a wave crashed around their feet.

Then he saw the art on the wall. The paintings were mostly Impressionistic; done in soft, romantic pastel colors. The prints were all in blues and greens, a nice touch with the plants. He glanced around the room. She did have a lot of plants – and for a second he thought of his mother, that she, like Severeen, had such a green thumb. He couldn't think about that. Not now. Not yet.

To distract himself he stood and examined a Monet print, "The Cliff Walk at Pourville," he knew it was called. It was amazing, the sense of calm he felt just from looking at it. The same calm the girls that Monet painted must have felt, just standing there above the vibrant water, watching the faint white sails in the distance, a sunny day with a breeze that tugged at their dresses and swept the blades of grass.

"I wish I had that view," Severeen said as she set silverware on the table.

"The one you have is nice," he said, glancing at the window, the lights brightening against the darkened city.

"That's pretty much what I pay for here." She motioned for him to sit and uncovered their meal. "I've never made it before, but I did follow the recipe, so there's hope."

Delan moved forward, curiously examining the dish.

"It's couscous. Cracked wheat and vegetables with beef sauce."

"It looks Kurdish."

"Does it? That's what I was hoping."

Severeen poured them each some wine, and then sat back as Delan served her first, and then piled food onto his own plate.

"The hospital gave me three days off. To help, you know. But getting you some more clothes, that won't take too long. Is there anywhere you'd like to go in Paris?"

Delan looked up, his fork in midair. "The Louvre, all the museums. But the Louvre first. Rodin's museum next."

"That one's actually pretty small, we could do it in the same day."

"It won't be boring for you?"

"Not at all. Look at my walls. I love art."

Though he didn't say anything, he studied her for a while then smiled and dug into his food. Saint Germain Des Pres Boulevard seemed to be crowded at all times and Delan seemed more interested in people-watching than finding clothing.

"Delan, this one," Severeen said, pointing to a door beside her. Reluctantly he turned towards the store. "All of Paris will still be here when we're done," she said, and nudged him towards the door.

Within what seemed like only minutes, Delan had found a few items and opted to wear his new outfit, bundling up his old clothes into a bag. The second they stepped back onto the boulevard and rounded a corner, Delan stopped by a homeless man and handed him the bag. The man looked up curiously, and without looking inside the bag thanked him with a nod.

The Metro would be a new experience for him, Severeen knew, and she watched him to make sure he was all right. Just like everyone else, he boarded the train and held on, though unlike everyone else, he was alert and taking in everything, his eyes moving up and down the compartment to the views outside and back to the people in the car.

His curiosity; his seemingly-famished gaze, only heightened at the Louvre. Never had Severeen been with someone so knowledgeable about art, and soon she discovered that watching him experience each piece was actually, in some cases, more interesting than the paintings themselves. "It's overwhelming," he said when – hours later – they left. "So many Great Masters in one place. It's stunning."

"Tomorrow we'll go to the Rodin museum," she said, steering him down a street. "Would you like to go the Champs-E'lysee? It's a boulevard, filled with expensive stores and incredible coffee shops." He shrugged and she continued. "And tonight we can have Greek food. Do you like it?"

Again he shrugged. "I've never had it."

Severeen motioned for him to cross the street, and thought how amazing it was to be with someone who'd not yet formed all the tastes and favorites they would ever have. She glanced at him, his head tilted towards the façade of a building, then turning quickly as a double decker bus drove by. She feared that the museum wasn't the only thing that was overwhelming.

***

The next day, after adding Greek food to his new list of loves, they took their time walking in the garden, looking at the Gate of Hell in Rodin's museum.

"My mother, she loved flowers. Plants. She could make anything grow."

Severeen nodded. He was talking about his mother in the past tense, which was difficult to hear. "That's how my mother was, too."

He glanced at her. "She's not, she's not here?""No, she passed away when I was young, very young. We couldn't keep up the garden though. Nothing we did seemed to work. We watered, we pruned. It was like the plants knew her touch and they didn't want much to do with us."

"My mother had a garden," he said, and Severeen realized what she'd done. He was now thinking of his mother's garden, untended, left to dry in poisoned air.

Inside the museum, they stopped before The Kiss. Silently they studied it, unable to take their eyes off it. They moved slightly to see it from different angles, to appreciate the curves of the marble, so smooth. Severeen studied the man's hand, languid on the woman's thigh, and tilted her head just slightly, right as Delan moved a few inches to the left. Startled, they both turned towards each other. There was a moment of silence. Delan's eyes had green in them.

"This one's my favorite," a man announced to his wife.

Embarrassed, Severeen and Delan stepped apart, but Severeen saw, just as he was turning away, a slight smile on Delan's face.

***

The ride home was silent. Severeen stared out her window, only once glancing towards Delan, preoccupied with the passing scenery. She heard of things like this happening, doctors and nurses developing feelings for the patients for whom they cared. "It's normal," she told herself, "There's nothing wrong with it. I just can't act on it.

Although she had felt the start of such feelings, it wasn't until today that she saw them returned in Delan's eyes.

"He feels the same," Severeen realized. But she wasn't sure if the knowledge was a comfort or a concern. Getting involved wasn't something recommended – especially not when the patient is still in the midst of a difficult and emotionally turbulent recovery.

Once more she glanced at him, and when she did she saw him turn, only slightly, but enough that he must have seen her looking, and then turn back again.

Walking up to her apartment, they were quiet. Each trying to decide the best course of action. Finally, Delan spoke.

"Would you like Kurdish food tonight?"

"Anything. I'm starving."

He paused in the hallway. "Great, I'll go to that market on the corner. Just need some spices, some eggplant..Do you like eggplant?"

"Sure. But I probably have things here,you should look first"

"I have ," he laughed, and then turned.

'All to get away from me," she thought, grateful for the break.

Alone in her apartment she sank into the sofa and stared at the ceiling. Being alone felt luxurious. The silence was not awkward. No reason to move, or speak.

What was she doing? Such different people, such a difficult situation.

When she heard the knock on the door, Severeen sat up, her heart rate increasing with more than just the movement. She liked him. There was no way around it.

She couldn't take the silence anymore. So she turned the radio to a classical station, and watched Delan unpack the groceries; lining everything up along the counter. He cleaned the meat, and put the ground lamb in a pan on the stove, then put all the vegetable on the chopping board.

"Will you teach me?" she asked, breaking the silence. "I don't have to do anything, Tell me what you're doing so I can learn?"

"First, preheat the oven. It's this here, with the knobs," he said, turning the oven on. She shook her head . He smiled, and handed her the bag of walnuts. "Chop these. Not too much, just into pieces. Right now I'm chopping the lamb, into chunks."

When he was ready to start work on the eggplant, he waited. The kitchen was small, and Severeen could tell he was waiting for her. Quickly she scooped the chopped walnuts into a little glass bowl, then wiped her hands on her pants.

"Next?"

"The eggplant. You want to make it hollow.
Like this," he demonstrated, chopping off the end. Severeen stood close to him, watching. So close he could smell her hair, her shampoo, a floral scent that was highly distracting. He had to concentrate, but all he could see was her arm, her hand, reaching for another eggplant.

With a spoon he began to carve the inside. "Like this," he said taking a step a way. Out of the corner of his eye he saw her turn to face him, just briefly, inquisitively. Grabbing an eggplant, and then another, Severeen moved to the chopping block on the other side of the kitchen, which suddenly seemed intimately small.

She stopped chopping. Something was burning. Spinning around she opened the oven door, releasing a black billow of smoke. "

"The pan!" Severeen pointed, prompting Delan to grab a potholder and reached inside the oven. Quickly she went to the sink, running the faucet as Delan shoved the cookware under the flow. Steam rose from where the water hit the hot metal.

"Now you see how much I love doing dishes," she chuckled, turning to open the window. But as Severeen reached to open the latch she felt herself being turned back around and embraced in a sudden, unexpected kiss.

Instinctively her shoulders relax and dropped as she felt his fingers, comb through her hair. And without protest, she willingly fell into his arms, even as the fire alarm's shrill blared though the smokey room.

When they finally broke apart, Delan grabbed the broom by the trash can, and began furiously waving it in front of the beeping, angry contraption on the wall. The shrill stopped as suddenly as it started and he turned back to her. "I've been wanting to do that for a while."

"What? Set off my alarm?", she smiled slyly. "I know. I've been resisting, too. It's so complicated, with you, my job, your family…"

New Beginning

"I have to go back there,", he stepped closer. "I have to see who's left."

"Of course,"

Gazing into each other's eyes, the silence spoke volumes. For a long moment the heat in the room rose until the recognizable 'whoosh' of a small fire turned their attention to the stove.

Quickly Delan reached passed Severeen, and lifted off the boiling pot lid, releasing the pressure. "I can see why you don't cook more often. This kitchen is cursed!"

"That's what I've been telling people," she laughed, switching off the stove's glowing eye, " but no one believes me."

"You said you had rice, right?"

"And... a bottle of wine I've been saving.'

***

"Good news," Dr. Beegee announced, knocking on Severeen's office door. Waving the check in his hand, he smiled broadly. "It's retroactive too."

"How much?"

"Twenty-five thousand francs. Not that much, but enough. More than I thought, actually. If he wants to find family, this is how he's going to do it."

Severeen smiled, not wanting to let on too much. But like any good doctor, Beegee could surmise the unseen.

"As a friend it's tough to see someone go through what Delan has. As more than a friend... Well. I don't have to tell you how hard it would be. You're a smart woman and I'm sure you've debated all this, so. All I'll do is point out that he has a rough road ahead of him. He has to go home, find what remains of his life."

"I know. It doesn't make any sense."

"Love rarely ever does."

***

"Seriously sis," Janine emphasized, taking the bowl of leftover rice and scooping some onto a plate. "Saddam is adding more and more troops to the Kuwaiti border. Would going to the South of France for a getaway be too boring?"

"It's not where Delan's life is. Or what's left of his life."

"Vacations with new loves are stressful enough. I can't believe you want to add murder and mayhem to your itinerary. Cause that's what you're doing, Literally!"

"I've decided to embrace the illogical and throw caution to the wind."

There was a knock on the door, followed by Delan turning the key and stepping inside.

"Delan," Severeen said, "you don't have to knock."

Delan nodded and greeted Janine.

"I'm watching your place while you're gone," Janine said. "It's perfect, I was about to kill my roommate."

"Don't you live with your boyfriend?" Delan asked, confused.

"Roommate, boyfriend. Anyone who eats the last of my ice cream and doesn't replace it – or leaves dirty socks on the sofa – is someone I could use a break from."

Delan took off his jacket, carefully hanging it on the back of the chair. "I met a Kurdish student today. He's going back to Kurdistan through Turkey. We'll travel with him. He's been back twice by crossing the Turkish border."

Severeen nodded, determined to keep her nerves hidden from her sister. "And that's safe, at least.""

"But that could change," Janine said. "Anything there could change. With everything going on with Kuwait?"

"Janine. Enough. Did I tell you we're taking the train?"

Janine's hand froze mid-air, a mound of rice wobbling slightly. "The Orient Express?"

"We still have to get our tickets. We're just waiting to make sure we can get the special passport Delan needs."

"And then just like that, you'll be gone."

Severeen laughed.

"Just like that."

The Orient Express

Standing at the train's window Severeen, watched the platform begin to slowly slide past. It appeared she was standing still while the world around her was gaining momentum. Behind her Delan unpacked a few things, then asked her to close her eyes. She sat in the little bench across from the bunk beds, beginning to feel the rumbling of the tracks as they picked up speed. "Still keep them closed?" she asked.

"Just a bit longer."

She nodded, though of course couldn't tell if he was looking at her or not. She couldn't believe she was doing this, but so far had told herself it was best not to think. Don't think. Just do. Not quite the best way to live life, but the best way at the moment.'

"Now. Open."

On the little table, by the window, was a bottle of wine and a single red rose laid between two glasses.

"Oh, almost forgot," he added, setting two blocks of cheese onto the table

"Shall I?" Severeen asked, picking up the bottle. Delan nodded and Severeen waited till the train had taken a corner, then poured just a bit into each glass.

"One more thing for you."

Severeen turned. On the bed was a box, wrapped in green and red paper.

"Christmas?"

"It was the only paper I found at your place."

"I'm kidding. That you even found wrapping paper is impressive." She slid open a corner, then gave up being graceful and ripped the paper, then pried open the box. Inside was a 35 mm camera.

"Delan, I needed this! How did you even notice?"

"I found that one in your closet. It wouldn't load film. So I knew you didn't have a working camera. And it was too big. Something hanging around your neck like that isn't good for traveling in the mountains. This one's perfect. I have film, too. In my bag."

Severeen cranked the tab. "There's film already." She picked up the camera and aimed it at Delan. He grinned, the scenery behind him a blur.

Within an hour they were plunging through country: passing small towns, stone houses and rolling hills of grapes and lavender. "I can see why impressionists were drawn here," Delan said.

"I picture Kurdistan beige - everything beige, with palm trees."

"That's how it is in southern Iraq, but not Kurdistan. It's different in the north. The mountains are green, covered with trees: Maples, Oaks, Aspens, Cottonwoods. Spring water rushes down the slopes, joins together, then heads down into the valley and south, where they become the Tigris and Euphrates, the cradle of civilization."

"Kurdistan is different than most of the Middle East. Though over time the invaders have cut many trees and cemented streams. Still, she's like a woman with scars, beautiful no matter. You fall in love with her, everyone does."

In the morning Delan sat by the window, letting Severeen sleep, watching a low fog roll over the lower slopes of the Alps. A trail of smoke rose steadily from a farmhouse in the distance, and a line of cows made its way towards a barn. White daisies sprinkled the hillsides.

Delan turned towards Severeen, still covered completely by her blanket.

"You're missing the Alps."

Severeen lowered the blanket. "It's cold!" Hesitantly she sat up. "It's foggy. Why are you up?"

"I couldn't sleep. These are all countries I've never been. I couldn't miss them." He stood up. "Come on. Let's get breakfast."

"Bathroom first."

Standing in line, they watched a dark, Middle Eastern looking man pass them. He paused at the end of the car, then leaned against the wall, looking out the window.

"What about your friend?" Severeen asked.

"Which friend?"

"The Kurdish one who was going to join us, traveling."

Delan nodded. "He's flying there. Change of plans. But he'll meet us in Diyarbakir in Kurdistan of Turkey and travel with us from there into Kurdistan of Iraq."

Severeen couldn't decide if the motion of the train was soothing or nauseating. "I smell coffee."

"We got the first stamp on our passports last night."

"I vaguely remember."

"Do you? I think you had your eyes closed."

Finally the bathroom door cranked open, and a tired, on edge looking woman emerged. "Third day on the train," the woman said. "Whoever says it rocks you to sleep is lying."

Severeen smiled and as she stepped inside the bathroom caught a glance of the Middle Eastern man, still standing at the end of the car, watching them. Quickly he looked back out the window, and Severeen closed the door.

***

Nearing the Turkish border, the Black Sea seemed to swell on the right side of the train. Both Delan and Severeen sat at a table in the dining car, coffee swaying dangerously in their cups. Again, the man from earlier was nearby, now only two tables away.

"Is he following us?" Severeen asked.

Delan didn't turn around, but nodded. "I'm not sure. He's probably fine, but just in case, watch what you say."

All throughout lunch Severeen watched the man, who leafed through a newspaper and then a magazine. He gazed now and then around the car in a way that seemed false. When they stood, Severeen caught his gaze above the pages of his magazine. He looked down, and Severeen took Delan's hand.

As soon as they were back in their compartment, Severeen locked the door. "Okay. I didn't want to admit it, but I'm scared." She paced by the window.

Delan laughed. "Not all Middle Eastern people are spies you know."

"But him? Everywhere we go he pops up."

Just for fun she went to the door and leaned in to the peephole. He was there. She stood back sharply, and stared at Delan, eyes wide. He looked at her questioningly and she nodded, motioning to the door.

In two steps Delan was at the door. The man stared at them, startled.

"Can I help you?" Delan said in English.

The man nodded and Severeen noticed he wasn't very tall, maybe 5' 8" at the most. He looked down at the ground as if to regain his composure. Severeen noticed a deep scar that stretched from the corner of his mouth to his chin.

When he looked up he smiled. "I'm sorry to bother you." His eyes flickered towards Severeen. "Where in Turkey are you going?"

She said nothing, but glanced at Delan.

Delan held up his hand. "It's alright Severeen." Then he turned towards the man. "We are going to Diyarbakir."

The man nodded quickly, furtively. He glanced again at Severeen, who started back towards the window. "Please. Let me introduce myself." But instead of saying more, he glanced back towards the hall. When he turned back, his voice was a whisper. "I'm a Kurd."

With that, Delan motioned for him to come inside. The man did so with a nod, then shut the door behind him. Severeen motioned for him to take a seat.

"Thank you. I'm sorry for all this, I must have made you two nervous. But I heard enough to convince me you were going to Kurdistan." He looked at Delan now. "You know how careful you must be, even to say 'Kurdistan'."

"Yes, I know. I didn't think we said Kurdistan, not lately."

"On the last train, from Paris."

"You came from Paris?" Severeen asked.

"I'm a teacher at the Sorbonne. Almas is my name."

"What do you teach?"

"Kurdish. So you can see why I'm so cautious. In Turkey, where we'll be, you can't speak the language at all. That is, unless you want to go to jail."

"I didn't realize they taught that there," Severeen admitted.

"Many years ago, at the Sorbonne, a Kurdish prince started teaching the language."

Delan looked up, surprised. "Who?"

"His name was Dr. Kamaron Bedirkhan."

"Oh." Delan nodded. "I've heard of the family. They were active in the Kurdish struggle early in the century?"

"Yes; very active, very smart, driven people. He was well-respected among the intellectuals, officials and nobility all throughout Europe. Especially Paris."

"I'm Delan," he said, extending his hand. "This is Severeen. Sorry, we just wanted to be sure who you were."

"I understand, especially when you are with someone." He smiled at Severeen. "I'm going to marry my fiancé and bring her back with me. You can't be too careful though." He paused, then looked up at Delan. "What border village are you crossing?"

"Silopi," answered Delan. "Ah. I have family there. Just outside of the city. They can help you, if you need it."

"Yes," Delan said. "That's very nice of you. It's always good to have more friends."

Almas stood. "I need to get back to my chamber before the immigration officials come knocking. I'll see you at the border." He stood at the door and peered through the peephole. Turning back once more, he nodded, then opened the door, looked down both ends of the hallway, and was gone.

***

Later that afternoon they ran into Almas in the dining car. Severeen motioned for him to join them, but it was only after quickly glancing around at the other passengers that he slid into the booth. "I was just telling Delan about Istanbul," Severeen said. "I'd love to spend some time there."

"Ah, a very historical city. Filled with exciting and mystifying things. The Islamic architecture will take your breath away. The mosques, the bazaars."

"I never asked you," Almas said quietly. "What part?" he hesitated, "what part are you from?"

Just as quietly, Delan answered, "Halabja."

Almas nodded. "I'm sorry. Your family?"

"Some are still there. Most didn't make it."

"And you, you weren't there?"

As Almas asked the question, Severeen noticed his eyes flicker towards Delan's face, the left side of which was still speckled with faint burn scars. "Yes, I was there."

Again, Almas just nodded. "It's easy for us to lose faith." He looked out the window. "The number three train is next for us."

At the station in Istanbul, Almas bought tickets for all three of them while Severeen reserved seats. The mix of people was striking. The fair skinned Europeans a stark contrast to the dark Turks.

"Here," Almas said when he met up with them. "From this point on no mention of where we're going or who we are."

"Thank you." Severeen took their tickets and slid them into her purse, feeling suddenly as if even possessing a ticket to Diyarbakir was dangerous.

"When we get to our destination, you two stay with me till your arrangements have been made."

"No," Delan said. "No, you are a guest yourself."

Almas smiled. "When I come to visit your town, you'll do the same. Besides, I want to talk freely with you, about things we cannot on the train."

They all fell silent, letting the rhythmic motion of the tracks carry them into contemplation, daydreams, and eventually sleep. This time they didn't have a private compartment. Severeen eyed the other passengers skeptically. Everything was fine, she was sure. But there was an edge to the feeling in the train, as if everyone knew to be on guard. Besides, Delan sat next her, his sketch book resting in his lap, his eyes shut. It made her nervous to be in the open like this, especially with Delan asleep. Who would notice if there was something were to happen? Thankfully, Almas looked lost in thought. His head leaned against the window, though each time a new cluster of people entered the car he looked up, alert.

When three quiet, Turkish men sitting in front of them stood and left their seats. Almas sat up. Severeen looked around nervously. Now anyone could sit there. It was the perfect place to study them or ask them seemingly innocent questions. For a while the seats remained empty. Then, three American soldiers entered the car, bringing with them a flurry of noise and commotion. They went straight for the empty seats.

Delan woke, glancing at Severeen and Almas to make sure everything was fine.

"Nice nap?" Severeen asked.

"Yes, I needed it." He looked down at his sketch pad. Then up at the blond American in front of him. His cheekbones were heavily pronounced, lending a gaunt, starved look to his face. Then Delan looked back down at his pad, and just like that began to trace an amazingly accurate depiction of the man's face.

"Time flew," the solider said.

"As it does when you're not miserable," said the man on his left.

They said nothing more for a bit, and then, as if uncomfortable with the silence, the blond man looked straight at Delan. "Where are you folks headed?"

"Diyarbakir," Almas answered for him.

The solider in the aisle seat, his head shaved, his skull seemingly dented in one place, studied them. "We're stationed a few miles outside there."

"At the air force base?" Almas asked.

"You know it?" the blond asked.

"Its my town. I'm Almas," he smiled. "These are my friends, Delan and Severeen."

"Nice to meet you," said the blond soldier. "I'm Billy. This here's Tom Crusse, not to be confused with Tom Cruise the actor, though they do fly about the same, which is to say shitty. And that's Ben McDonald."

Ben, the one with the dented skull, nodded. "Nice to meet you."

"McDonald, were you tortured by the song? Or the restaurant?"

Ben smiled. "Both, equally. You're Parisian?"

"Yes, I'm from Paris."

"Figured," Ben said. "Just about everyone I know from France is from there. Maybe the folks in the country don't travel much?"

Severeen laughed. "I have no idea."

Billy smiled at Severeen. "Severeen, did I say that right? Are you going to Diyarbakir too?"

Almas answered for her. "Yes. She and Delan are both my guests."

With that, everyone glanced at Delan, as if just remembering he was there. Tom leaned forward. "Holy shit. Billy, it's you. Look."

Delan smiled, then handed the sketchbook over.

Billy studied his face intently.

"You're good man. Is this is your bag?"

"No, my bag is over there," Delan pointed.

"I meant do you do *this* for a living? Billy smiled.

Delan nodded.

"Where you from?" Tom asked.

Almas, Severeen and Delan all were quiet for a moment, and Severeen could feel them collectively assessing the situation. Finally, Delan spoke. "Iraq."

"So, you're an Arab." Tom said. Though he was smiling as he spoke, Severeen did not like where he was going.

"No," Delan offered, surprisingly. "I'm a Kurd."

For a while, no one spoke. Almas turned, studying the car as if making sure no one had moved, and that the announcement had not set off alarms.

"A Kurd," Billy said. "Man! What they did to your people."

"Thank you," Delan nodded.

"That Saddam!" Tom grimaced.

Immediately both Delan and Almas raised their hands to silence him.

"Shh," Almas warned. "Do not talk of him. Especially around us."

"Sorry," Tom continued, in a practical whisper. "But he put four hundred thousand soldiers and four hundred tanks on the Kuwaiti border. Don't tell me he's not about to invade that little ass country."

"Jesus, Tom," Billy gestured to Severeen. "We got a lady here. And, you're behind in the news. Hussein's in Kuwait. Happened today."

Delan and Almas looked at each other. "With the money from the Kuwaiti oil," Almas said, "he'll build an unstoppable army. First, the Emirates, then Saudi Arabia. Then the rest of the Middle East."

Tom shook his head. "Oh! No he won't. Bush warned him."

"Won't stop him," Ben declared. "First he kills Kurds and Shiites. Then he takes over his neighbors. He wants to be the leader of all Arab countries. The man's a genuine threat."

"He'll never be another Saladin," Delan observed. "Saladin was a Kurd, who united all of Islam. To do that you have to have respect for human life. Hussein, doesn't."

Almas' eyes widened, and directed his new friends attention to a man in a dark suit, headed towards them. Nonchalantly, the stranger took a seat less than five feet away. The talkative group fell silent.

***

The next morning, everyone awoke in the same places. The soldiers, accustomed to finding sleep anywhere, used duffel bags as pillows. Severeen lifted her head from Delan's shoulder. It was quiet. The whole train seemed asleep. Outside, the light was barely present, as if a dial had only been turned just a bit.

"Sleep well?" Delan whispered.

"I didn't mean to wake you," she whispered back.

"I've been awake. I just didn't want to move, you looked so comfortable." He leaned across Severeen, towards the window, he nodded. "We're close to Diyarbakir."

"Only minutes," Almas added, his eyes still shut.

Delan laughed. "How do you know, you're talking in your sleep."

"Maybe. But I can also see in my sleep." He opened his eyes. "I haven't slept all night."

Before them, Billy stretched, disturbing the line-up and waking his friends. "Man, what I wouldn't do to be back on base."

"Bed," Tom yawned. "My bed misses me. At home though, not the one on base."

Ben shook his head. "Hey, if we're gonna start dreaming I'll be at the Four Seasons. Got about as much chance of being there as we do our own beds."

"You're the smart ass who said there was no point in traveling First Class," Tom punctuated, with a well-placed elbow punch.

Soon everyone in the car was up, gathering bags, stretching, peering out windows as the city limits enveloped them. When the train stopped, a crowd awaited.

Delan turned to the soldiers. "It was nice traveling with you."

Tom reached out to shake his hand. "Likewise man."

"Remember what we talked about," Almas reminded the young men. "Tell people. We're not the bad guys. We're an ancient people. We just want peace, and we need help."

The soldiers nodded, and soon the group was caught in the determined flow of people exiting the train.

Diyarbakir

The moment Severeen stepped off the train she spotted Almas' fiancé; a woman of dark exotic beauty, with hair as black as pitch. And as Almas appeared in the doorway, Severeen watched with delight as the waiting woman's eyes brightened with recognition. Within seconds the two were together, joined at the lips.

"Where's the family?" He asked in English, mindful of Severeen.

Hearing his choice in language his fiancée smiled at Severeen and hugged her man closer. "I ran ahead for a kiss."

"I'm Severeen," she returned the smile, "And this, "she gestured to the approaching man, "is Delan."

"We met on the train," Almas explained. Then, hugging the exotic beauty closer he declared proudly, "My friends, this is Ronak, my fiancé."

"A pleasure," Delan nodded. "He has spoken of nothing but you. The whole train ride, nothing but 'Ronak!"

Her olive eyes turned to Almas with admiration. "Good."

As they spoke, a large happy group descended on the foursome. And amid the chaos of greetings and embraces, Almas laughed, "And this the family!"

When the delightful attack subsided, Almas turned to his new friends and gestured respectfully to the two oldest members of the greeting party. "Friends, I'd like to introduce my mother, Golnaz and my father, Sofe Hamed." And looking in his parents' direction he added, "These are my friends, Severeen and Delan. I have invited them to be our houseguests."

The old man studied Delan for a moment. Then, in halting English, he nodded his approval. "You are welcome," and quietly added a phrase in Kurdish.

Delan smiled, turned to Severeen, and whispered. "He says he hopes we enjoy our stay."

Grinning gratefully in the elder's direction, Severeen replied under her breath, "Imagine; not being able to speak your own language."

In the parking lot, the group headed to an old Mercedes and a small Italian car. Pointing to the Mercedes, Hamid motioned for Severeen to take the front seat. "Oh, no," she said.

"Please," Hamid said and motioned once again.

Severeen watched half the family climb into the smaller car, and looked back at Delan. He smiled, and leaned in close. "You'll notice," he said quietly, "we treat visitors very well. And it's an insult to protest." With that, she climbed inside, and smiled. Once the doors shut, everyone broke into Kurdish.

The cars snaked their way through the winding streets of the city. Severeen was mesmerized by the ancient buildings still standing they passed along the way.

Diyarbakir was a historic trade center between the Far East and the Middle East, surrounded by very thick black, basalt walls, several miles long. The city was built in the Fourth Century by the Constantine Empire. And in the Fifteenth Century, it was captured by the Ottoman Empire. The Kurds have always considered Diyarbakir as the unofficial capital of Kurdistan North.

As they arrived, entering the family home, two of Almas' sisters stood. Both were tall, with intensely dark, bewitching eyes. Each were exotically beautiful in a way that made Severeen realize that beauty was not uncommon among the Kurds. One, Freshta, was just in college, and the other, Nazaneen, was only sixteen, but already as tall as her mother.

Ronak introduced her family, who had also gathered for the homecoming. Severeen nodded, greeting each one, not sure if she should shake hands or not. Roshan leaned in warmly and gave her a kiss on both cheeks.

Soon, Ardy, Almas' younger brother, carried in a tray with tea and little glass teacups. At almost six feet tall, he was the tallest in the room, and had some of the most brilliant hazel eyes Severeen had ever seen. Almas pointed to the dining room, where more people stood and chatted.

"In there is my older sister Payman. She's married to the man standing next to her, Faraydoon Ezat. He is a school teacher."

As if aware they were being watched, Payman and a couple other women turned and nodded at the group, then went back to arranging food on a table.

Eventually dinner was ready and everyone sat at the table, with the exception of Ronak's parents, who apparently preferred the doshak, or futon. They said something in Kurdish, which Delan translated. "They want to know if we would like to join them."

Severeen nodded, and she and Delan arranged themselves on the doshak. Within seconds a large tray of food was set in front of them on the floor, and then another large tray was set on the table. Everywhere, it seemed, there was food. When everyone in the room began eating, Severeen looked to Delan for clues as to how to eat. Carefully he tore a piece of flat bread and scooped rice and lamb onto it, making a sort of open-faced sandwich.

Sofe, Almas' father, watched Severeen from the table. "I hope you enjoy the way we eat," he said. "This is very traditional."

"I've never been outside France, so new traditions, new cultures, all of it I love."

Sofe nodded, then whispered something to Almas who smiled, and turned to Delan. "My father asks if you would stay for my wedding. The wedding party will be small, but fun."

Severeen glanced at Delan and said, "Let's stay. I've never seen a Kurdish wedding,"

"My friend is supposed to be here tomorrow," he paused to tear off a piece of bread. He shook his head in agreement. "We're suppose to travel together. Maybe he will stay for a couple days."

"So, you will stay?" Almas raised his eyebrows, expectantly.

"Sure. We'd love to be here for your wedding."

"Good!" Sofe clapped his hands in celebration, "Now, eat more!"

***

The next day they sat outside with Almas' parents and sisters. The patio was framed with bright fragrant flowers. But despite the pleasant surroundings, no one appeared happy.

"Your life, your family" Sofe, finally broke the silence, looking in Delan's direction. "So tragic." Then turning from his houseguest, he sat silent for a moment, slowly turning his gaze up to the clear, empty sky, he voiced the question everyone was thinking, "Why? "Why do you do this to us?" The old man's frustration was loud, deliberate. "Why must the Kurds endure this? What have we done?"

With a sense of resignation he looked down and studied his hands, tanned heavily lined from work.

No one said a word. After a while old Kurd looked back up at Delan.

"Maybe God is looking after you, my son. We should be thankful you are still alive and well. It's sad that in our history, only the tragic parts repeat themselves again and again."

Severeen took Delan's hand, and gave it a little squeeze.

"My father was going to the University of Istanbul," Sofe offered, studying his now folded hands. "He left his family, his parents, his four brothers and three sisters, to be an engineer. Not long after he left, the Kurdish holocaust began. Attaturk ordered the death of hundreds of thousands of Kurds. Thousands were put in brown bags and thrown into Lake Van, alive. Thousands were hanged. In the city of Van there was a Kurd dangling from every tree."

Shaking his grey head, he looked up at his silent, attentive guests. "In Diyarbakir and Darsim, thousands of innocent families were put in caves and sealed in with concrete. When my father was able to return from university, he found he had only one sister left. All of his family was gone."

"The atrocities," Sofe continued, gazing deep into Severeen's eyes, "There seems to be no end to what is done to us. Thousands of years of culture they tried to destroy. Our language. Our music." He turned to Severeen. "Our music is banned you know."

Severeen nodded, not sure how else to respond to tales of such pain and desperation. Her discomfort compounded with each of Sofa's descriptive words, pushing her anxiety beyond its usual borders. And she was thankful when he finally broke his gaze, looked away and smiled.

"But we never lose hope. Only God knows what tomorrow will bring. We know we will never stop our struggle until they respect us, until they treat us like human beings." He laughed, sadly. "We're not asking for much. Just to be treated like human beings."

***

A while later, after tea on the patio, and more food, Delan dialed the hotel where his friend was planning to stay. As the phone rang, Almas grabbed the receiver out of Delan's hand. "Let me talk. My Turkish is better. "Yes, may I speak with – " he paused, looking to Delan.

"Hewa Ahmad," Delan whispered.

"Hewa Ahmad," Almas repeated, "Thank you."

Then, with a sense of accomplishment, he handed the phone to Delan whispering, "They're connecting you." After a moment Delan heard his friend's deep voice. "Hewa! It's Delan." He spoke in Kurdish, a risk he knew. "I'm glad you called."

"What's happening?

"I have some bad news. You know the situation in Iraq, I'm sure. I need to see you. We must talk...in person."

Delan's heart sank. "Yes. We're going on a tour of the city for a few hours. How about some time after three o'clock?"

"Make it three thirty at the café down the street from the hotel."

As he hung up the phone, he saw his anxiety mirrored on Severeen's face. And realizing, he feigned a smile "Go with Ronak. Change into some comfortable clothes... It's okay."

***

Throughout the city tour, Severeen fought to focus on her surroundings and banish all the worry of what may be to come. Knowing Delan's friend would deliver bad news, she tried to savor her few hours of ignorance, and pretend that exotic architecture, fragrances and faces were all that mattered.

Entering the coffee shop, Severeen hung back just a bit, following Delan, Almas and Ronak to a table in the corner. But the trepidation Severeen anticipated seemed unfounded the moment Hewa was introduced to her. His smile was broad and inviting as he engulfed her in a hug.

And after greeting Ronak with the same enthusiasm, the smiling man pulled two chairs out for the women as the men settled themselves in at the table.

"How do you like Diyarbakir?" he asked in slow but perfect English.

"Spread out," Delan laughed. "A long tour, but worth it."

"And you?" Hewa turned to Severeen.

"It's definitely different than Paris. Everything's fascinating - but we missed the market. I'd love to go there."

"Shopping," Hewa said with a smile. "Does not matter where you're from, women love to shop. Am I right?"

Severeen and Ronak glanced at each other, then laughed, sheepishly agreeing.

"So Delan and Severeen," he continued. "Your trip? Tell me how it was."

"Good," Delan said. "We were lucky to meet Almas. So far all is well. No problems."

"No problems, yet," Almas interrupted. "But the day is young."

Now Hewa's face turned serious. "Yes. Our contact is not here yet. I expect there are difficulties at the border. The Americans are moving in hundreds of thousands of troops, with NATO and the UN's baking,

. "It's not safe to talk about this here," Almas whispered, glancing around the café. His eye's then turned to Delan. "You can't leave until things are clear. Saddam is stubborn. He won't leave Kuwait until he's forced out – And force means war."

"Leave? You can't leave," Ronak interrupted. Her serious tone then brightened with a smile. "At least until after our wedding."

"Ah," Hewa grinned. "And when is that?"

All was silent as a tray of dark, mud-like coffee was placed before them. The amazing aroma enticed Almas to take a quick, appreciative sip before speaking.

"The wedding is in a week – on Newros – but the reception is tonight. We'll be partying until the wedding day. You know," pausing for another sip, he leaned in, and continued in a quieter tone. "Some of my relatives will be here from the border village. You'll meet them. They could help you cross."

"Thank you," Hewa spoke for the rest. "But we must wait for our contact."

"Ezamalden," Almas continued, "my father's cousin, was a teacher A nice man. One of his daughters is married to a Kurd on the Iraqi side of the border. Zakhu."

"They must cross all the time, then." Delan interjected, hopefully..

"The Turkish army killed his older son for sympathizing with the PKK " Almas whispered, coaxing Severeen to lean across the table. "He lives with his two youngest sons and one daughter. *He will help.*"

"We'll see how the next few days go," Hewa nodded, "but we need to stop this talk. The walls have ears. And I must leave to meet a friend."

"Severeen," Almas spoke up, changing the subject. "Perhaps something a bit lighter is in order now. Would you like to go to the market? It's only blocks from here." Without waiting for her to agree, he glanced at Delan. "Talking there is safer."

***

The market was a whirl of fragrances and colors; wild rose, lavender, cumin, and cinnamon, all with a physical backdrop of bright reds and golds. Fabrics hung in shop windows, jars of teas glinted in the sun. Delan watched as Severeen peered through windows, appreciating this world in a way he had long forgotten.

"I could stay here the rest of my life," she said as they entered a textile and rug store.

Almas, walking a few paces ahead, laughed. "You wouldn't say that if we took you to the area where they sell meat."

Severeen ran her fingers over a rug on a table. The weave was exquisite, the colors bold. Beside her Ronak found a smaller rug. And though she clearly liked it, she stood back so as not to show too much interest. Still, the owner of the shop inched closer.

"The designs," Severeen said to Ronak. "Do they mean something?"

Ronak glanced at the rug. "That is a tribal Kurdish creation. You should see them dyeing their yarn. It is a long, beautiful process."

The owner, clearly having heard, sidled up a bit closer. "You are French?" he asked Severeen, breaking the ice, "I studied in Grenoble. Marketing."

"Small world," Severeen sighed.

"Let me show you a rug," He motioned leading her to the back of the store. Delan, though not following, watched them closely.

Lifting half a stack of rugs the man carefully wedged out a sample, about three-by-five feet. The colors were brilliant, with vibrant reds and blues. "My sister," the man said quietly, his eye on the security guards outside his window, "best Kurdish rug maker in whole world. You are with Kurds, am I right?"

He didn't let her answer, which was fine with Severeen, for she knew not to say anything.

"I am Kurd," he admitted, softly but with a measure of pride. "I want to live as a Kurd and die as a Kurd." He smiled, then handed the rug to Severeen. "Have I said too much?"

Severeen grinned slightly. "You didn't tell me how much it is."

"It's yours." he nodded, "Don't argue."

Severeen shook her head handing the rug back. But the man held his hands up in protest.

"No, I can't," she said, "really."

"You must." Then his voice dropped to a whisper again. "Tell the French people about the rug makers. The Kurds."

Looking into his sincere eyes, she knew she could not refuse the gesture. "Thank you. I will cherish this. It means a lot to me, your kindness."

The shop owner's face reddening a bit from the compliment, and backed away just as her companions approached. "It's beautiful,' Delan declared, running his hand of the textured rug, "I know where this was made."

"Yes," Severeen nodded. "He told me."

"A bag," the owner offered. "And my card." Then he turned to Almas and Delan and whispered a greeting in Kurdish. They each, likewise, returned the greeting with a smile of confirmation.

Once outside, Almas leaned in close to Severeen. "He gave that to you?"

"Yes," she nodded. "In exchange I'm to tell the French people about the Kurds in Turkey."

"The familiar symbols in that rug make your present more than art," Almas revealed. "It's massage of unity should be displayed not only in a museum gallery, but in the headlines of every newspaper. "

Severeen clutched her bag tighter. "I can't believe he gave it to me."

"You will find the generosity of the Kurds is like nothing you've ever known. They will give you the shirt off their backs if you need it, or even if you want it."

They stopped in the area where the copper and bronze smiths set up shop. Everything gleamed with reflection of the mid day sun. Delan picked up a plate of both copper and bronze, and Severeen stood close to him, inspecting a vase.

"You like the market?" he asked her.

"I love the market."

Glancing behind him, he quickly leaned in and kissed her on the cheek. "I love you, too."

***

Once in the car, Almas glanced at Severeen through the rearview mirror. "I'd like to know more about that rug merchant."

"He gave me his card," she offered, handing it to Delan, sitting in the front seat.

"He seemed like a nice man," Almas continued. "He studied business in Grenoble he said."

Almas nodded. "I like his Kurdish spirit. A brave man."

The next day Almas was on the roof of his house, adjusting a handmade antenna. From the ground Delan watched. The sky behind his friend was a piercing blue.

"It's working!" Sofe called from the side of the house. Then, spotting Delan, he smiled proudly. "Almas always knows what to do to fix it," he said, and then disappeared back inside.

"What did you do?" Delan asked as Almas climbed back down.

"Nothing."

"Can you keep a secret?"

"Of course."

"Our neighbors raise white doves. They're beautiful, but they land on our antennae and there goes our reception. All I do is go up there and move it to how it was before those birds needed a place to sit."

Once back inside, Severeen met them at the door, Almas smiled and motioned them down a hallway. "This house has secret hiding place. It's not as exciting as it sounds. It's because of the laws here.

You can't be Kurdish. If they catch you celebrating of any kind – music, reading books, speaking the language, even talking about your ancestors – you're thrown in jail or worse. But who wants to get rid of all their memories? All their cherished books and music?"

"My father used to bury all his Kurdish books under the ground, so they'd be safe." Delan remembered. "Then one day he wanted a reference, so he started digging. When he got to them they were covered in mildew and damaged from water. All the books he cherished throughout his life, books that belonged to his father, and his father's father, all ruined. The look on his face. It was as if he'd lost one of his children. He didn't say anything. He didn't need to say anything."

They turned into a room and Almas immediately went to the window and drew the curtains. Once the room was dark and no longer visible from the street, he stopped before a china cabinet.

"My father couldn't lose any more. So he built this." With that he leaned into the cabinet, pushing it off the rug. Carefully he rolled it up revealing a trapdoor beneath. There was no railing on the stairs, and the room was dark, so Severeen and Delan stepped slowly leaning against the wall. When Almas reached the bottom he turned on a lamp, and the room appeared.

"If we had a room like this," Delan marveled, admiring a wall covered with book shelves, "we could've saved so much of our history, or memories." Turning to Severeen, who stood at a small wooden table supporting a shortwave radio. "We lost photos of Sheik Saied, Kazi Mohammed, and Barzani. So many."

Almas took a seat on a round cushion by the lamp. "No one but immediate family knows about this room."

"This radio works?" Severeen asked.

"It does now that I fixed the antennae." Almas smiled. "My father listens to the news in here, from all different countries. Good or bad about the Kurds, he wants to hear it. Not that the world has much to say about the Kurds.

Delan ran his fingers along the spines of the books, pausing now and then to read a title. "And Turkey is a NATO member," he said, glancing back at Severeen. "Yet none of the NATO nations speak up on behalf of the Kurds. Iraq and Syria are pro-Soviet Union, so there goes all the Soviet Blocks. Iran, the religious fanatics, they're going backwards with a human rights record that is shameful. And the US, they'll do whatever the Turkish government asks them to do – just like Iran before the revolution. So that leaves us, 24 million Kurds living every day on the verge of annihilation."

"The irony," Almas said, "is that the Turkish system is democratic. We have parliamentary elections. But the Kurds have no representation. And even if we had Kurds in Parliament, they couldn't speak on behalf of the Kurds. They'd be arrested for even *mentioning* the Kurds. I ask you, what is a democracy without freedom or peoples' rights?"

Delan pulled a small chair out from the table and motioned for Severeen to sit. Then he took a seat on the floor, leaning back against the wall. "The problem is they don't recognize that the Kurds exist. They say there are no Kurds, only mountain Turks who have lost their language."

"And yet, the Kurdish civilization her goes back thousands of years," Almas retorted. "Right here on this very land. The Turks of middle Asia invaded our country, slaughtering men, women and children. Over and over again for centuries they did this. Here, they initiated a genocide against both the Kurds *and* the Armenian people in the late eighteenth, and early nineteenth centuries. And they still use policy to melt the Kurdish nationalism, to try and turn us into Turks. If you refuse - if you stand up for yourself -for your ancestors - you can be deported, torn from your family and called a terrorist. Just for saying you're a Kurd you can be killed."

"It amazes me," Severeen gasped, "that I didn't know this. That this isn't common knowledge, that it's not talked about."

"It doesn't do other countries any good to talk about it. If they don't benefit, then why should they care?"

"Years ago," Almas reminisced, scanning the radio dial, "my father would search for stations with international news, turning the knob from one end to the other, for hours, hoping to hear some good news about the Kurds."

As he spoke, he turned the radio on, the volume low. "There were few stations that talked about us, but still he listened every day, hoping. So this day he stopped on some Middle Eastern talk show. My father, he speaks Arabic a little. On this show they were talking about life and death and someone called into the station and asked if there was a heaven or a hell. The radio man said he didn't know, then paused. Then he started laughing, 'But wait, if anyone knows about heaven and hell, it's Mostafa Barzani, the leader of the Kurdish resistance in Iraq. Several times during the sixties, when the Iraqi Army was fighting the Kurds, the Iraqi radio stations announced Barzani's death, hoping to break the hearts and will of the Kurds. According to the stations, he died *several* times. We should ask him! He's the expert!'"

Delan and Severeen laughed, and in the brief moment of silence that followed they heard the soft voice on the radio say the word *Iraq*. Almas quickly adjusted the volume.

"The United Nations coalition forces, spearheaded by the Bush administration, attacked Saddam Hussein's forces. The Air force having cut the supply route from Baghdad to Basra once Hussein, retreated from Kuwait. Meanwhile, Baghdad is under fire from the air, with the UN Coalition forces attempting to destroy all the Iraqi military and air force bases.

Baghdad glows like a fire at night from the heavy bombardment. Many buildings in the center of the city have been destroyed, including the two main and crucial bridges that connect the two sides of the city. In other parts of the country, the Shiite people of the South have taken control of all the southern cities, while in the north the Kurds have taken control. And now we take a break to look at..." Almas turned the volume down once more, then looked up at the stairs where his father stood.

"The victims," Sofe said, "are all poor people. They are losing their homes. They'll have nowhere to live. Thousands of innocent men, women and children will starve Earlier, I heard a report that General Schwarzkopf and the coalition forces were just outside of Baghdad. Why have they stopped? Why don't they go in and get Saddam, and put an end to all this? Finish the job." He shook his head, and turned for the door. "Come upstairs now. Enough politics, you have a future wife who needs help."

Severeen and Delan followed Sofe . Almas waited till they reached the top of the stairs before shutting off the light, Once back by the china cabinet, Delan and Almas straightened the rug as Severeen stood by the door. "Doesn't all this mean that the borders will get worse?" she asked.

"The Turkish forces," Sofe said, standing by the covered windows, "are patrolling all the borders between Iraq and Turkey. You will have to wait and see the outcome. I don't want anyone jeopardizing their lives."

"Still with politics?" Ronak grinned, appearing in the threshold of the room.

"You want to talk about the wedding," Almas motioned her closer. "Then we will. I have one more quest for you. The rug merchant we met."

"I thought so. Give me his card or I'll forget."

Almas agreed. Then both he and Delan dragged the cabinet back into its spot on the rug. Once everything was put back together, Sofe opened the curtains, filling the room with light.

***

The next day, as everyone sat in the living room discussing the wedding, there was a knock at the door. Everyone turned.

It's my musician friend!" Ardy realized, . I asked him to come by." Shrugging his shoulder in a clumsy apology for not mentioning the visitor earlier, he then opened the door!. "Come in! Come in. Long time no see."

With curiosity the group watched as a tall young man with pale skin and bright green eyes crossed the threshold. "Everyone, this is Aziz. He plays mostly Kurdish instruments and is quite popular."

The young man's cheeks reddening with sudden embarrassment, "No, no. I'm not that good. Not when I'm playing Turkish music."

"I've heard his Kurdish music," Almas interrupted. "In secret of course. He brings tears to your eyes. He's so good. One day," he pointed to the musician, with assurance, "you will be able to play your Kurdish melodies to the crowds."

"Are you playing at our wedding?" Ronak asked.

Aziz nodded. "I was planning on that."

Then his eyes went to the hall, where Freeshta emerged, holding a tray of tea. Her eyes quickly found him in the room, but she looked away so quickly that Severeen immediately looked back at Aziz just in time to see him redden again with a faint blush. Freeshta set the tray of tea on the table, and quietly took a seat in the corner of the room, keeping her eyes to the ground.

"Aziz, we haven't seen you in a while," Nazaneen said, rather playfully. "Wasn't it two years ago you promised to teach me to play the violin?"

"The violin!" Ardy said. "Why on earth that?" Nazaneen shook her head at her brother. "How could you ask that? The violin is beautiful. Such a sad sound. It takes you to other worlds, other dimensions."

"You only say that from having found that European classical station on the radio." "So? What's wrong with that?"

"I like the violin," Freeshta said. Everyone turned to her. "I do. And there's nothing wrong with learning a musical instrument, or learning different music all together."

"There," Nazaneen said. "You see? There's nothing wrong with it. Freeshta, maybe you'd like to learn with me?"

Now Freeshta shifted a bit in her seat, looking at her sister and then back down at the floor. "Yes, I would like that."

"Well then," Aziz said. "I shall teach you both. And I always keep my promises, even if it takes years."

Somewhere in the house a door slammed, and then Sofe appeared in the living room. "The Allied Forces are pulling out of Iraq and letting Saddam get away."

The room was silent. Finally, Delan spoke, sadly and yet optimistically. "Maybe he'll step down."

"No," Almas said. "And if he did he would be replaced by someone else in the Ba'ath party."

Sofe sat heavily in the closest chair. "Saddam is too much of an egomaniac to step down. If he survives this he will survive anything. Besides, who in his party would ask him to step down? No one would. Everyone is afraid of him."

Delan leaned forward to pour a cup of tea, but when he sat back he didn't take a sip. Instead, he simply nodded in agreement to what Sofe said. "He has one out of five people spying on the others. If anyone refuses to be an informer he kills them. Everywhere there are informers. Even in families. Family members don't trust each other. It's a tactic that has paralyzed the entire Iraqi population. He's turned everyone in the country against each other.

The Anfal (spoils of war) for example, was aimed at the Arabization of Kurdistan and demoralizing the Kurds. In the process he killed hundreds of thousands of Kurdish families or took them from their homes and towns and replaced them with Arabs. No one loves the family who just took their home, whether it was their choice or not."

Aziz smiled. "I don't know if this is a true story or not, but once Saddam was talking to his commanders and said 'We've done everything to destroy the Kurds and yet they still fight back.' To that one of the commanders stood up and said he had a solution. 'I know the Kurds very well,' he said, 'and the Kurds love art and music and they *love* to dance. Instead of killing them physically, why don't we give them drums and clarinets and let them dance themselves to death!'"

Only a few people laughed, and Aziz stood up to pour himself some tea. "Well," he said as he dropped a sugar cube into his cup, "I hope everyone here dances their hearts out at the wedding."

"We will," Sofe said with a wink, "especially if some Kurdish music makes it into the wedding."

Aziz nodded. "I wish we had drums, Dahol and Zorna Clarinets. But I have a very good tape which was recorded in a remote village. Two of the finest folk musicians alive." He smiled proudly. "I just got it two days ago."

"Let's listen!" Ronak said. "Can we go downstairs?"

Sofe stood up, pointed to the secret room, as he

looked at his wife. "You stay up here to make sure no one comes in."

Once downstairs, Aziz saw the shortwave radio and turned it on. "Much is happening. Do you mind?"

"Not at all," Sofe offered "Here, I'll find something." After turning the knob for a while, skipping through stations of varying static, he came across the voice of a British man. "In a moment," Sofe said. "Give it a moment and we'll see."

After listening to reports from around the world, the subject they had been waiting for came up.

"...Kurdish forces battling troops loyal to Saddam Hussein claimed control of wide areas of the Kurdish region in rugged northern Iraq, as opposition forces in several parts of the country reported new military gain. Radio reports in Turkey and Iran acknowledged heavy fighting in the Kurdish districts along their borders with Iraq, A Kurdish radio monitored by the British Broadcasting Company appealed for discipline among people living in areas it said were now in rebel hands. In the southern part of the country, near Basra, Shiite opposition forces reported that the key provincial city of Hillah, located sixty miles south of Baghdad had fallen to the Shiite forces, who executed several local officials loyal to Hussein."

As the voice faded into static, Sofe turned down the volume. "I can try Baghdad, but there's heavy static most of the time." Slowly he adjusted the knob, stopping on the crackly voice of a man speaking Arabic.

As the report came through, Delan translated as best he could for Severeen.

"The government announced it would open prison doors and release Iraqi inmates, all but those imprisoned for the most serious offenses." He paused, listening and leaned in close to the radio, "Under the decree the pardon includes all except prisoners convicted of spying, currency violations, rape, counterfeiting, premeditated murder, and crimes that impose the death penalty as punishment." He straightened, shaking his head at Severeen. "There go all the prisoners. They don't sentence political prisoners as political prisoners. They punish them under other crimes. They are the last to be freed."

Sofe motioned for Delan to listen. Once again Delan leaned in close to the radio and translated the report. "An official of the Iraqi Ministry of Information released a statement denying reports that there had been street battles inside the capitol between anti government demonstrators and soldiers." Another pause as a slew of Arabic unfolded. "The government radio broadcast described the reports as fabricated, and attributed them to a hostile and aggressive campaign waged by those against Iraq and its steadfast people."

As the reports ended, Sofe turned off the radio; "According to Iranian radio, most of the south and Kurdistan is controlled by opposition."

"That's what we heard, too," Severeen confirmed

"Yes, yes. Good to hear it wasn't just one report.

The Kurds invited foreign journalists to visit what they're calling a liberated Kurdistan."

Almas laughed. "So that's why the Turkish army is on total alert at the border? They're worried about the affect on our people, that the Kurds in Kurdistan of turkey will not get any ideas."

"Listen," Sofe turned to Delan with a serious tone. "The wedding is only in a couple days. After that I know you will want to leave. But there's heavy fighting near our border. Ten cities in the Dohuk area, close to the Turkish border, were taken over just yesterday by the Kurdish forces. The "opposition", as they call the Kurds, stormed the government offices and apparently now control key roads in the area. It sounds good. But it will be challenged. I beg you to wait until the Turkish troops relax on the border."

Delan glanced at Severeen, then back to Sofe and nodded, assuaging the old man's fears. But as Severeen watched her companion's silent act, she wasn't sure if he meant it.

***

March 21st, Newros, the Kurdish New Year, was the day picked for the wedding. And this year, not only would the New Year and the wedding be celebrated, but it seemed that the liberation of the Kurdistan of Iraq would also be cause of celebration.

"Never in my dreams did I think this day would come," Almas said. "My wedding *and* the freedom of Kurdistan, all falling on Newros."

Delan, Almas and Sofe sat outside, while the women and other family members gathered inside waiting for the festivities to begin. Ronak stayed at home a couple days prior to the wedding to make last minute repairs to the clothing that would used in the wedding. Bright, vibrant colored fabrics were spread about in her living room.

"According to Cairo radio," Sofe sighed, "the US officials said they were skeptical of the Kurds' claim to have taken control of Kirkuk, a major city of Kurdistan of Iraq. Without Kirkuk, we are still fighting."

"Saddam won't give up easily," Delan acknowledged. "Not with all the oil in Kirkuk."

March 19, 1991

Two days before the wedding Alma's mother and her two daughters were busy preparing for the big festivity with the help of their Aunt Shamsa. They could have used Ronak's help but in customary Kurdish tradition, the bride stays home until the wedding day.

Leaping up the stairs, Almas burst out of the secret basement, straight up the stairs to the roof, muttering, "Damned pigeons! Why don't they stay away from my father's radio antenna?" Hurriedly adjusting the antenna, he rushed back down to the stairs.

Sofe sat in front of his shortwave radio listening intensely as his son ran back into the room. Still focused, the old man thanked Almas, then directed his attention back to the radio and the voice of an Iranian station newscaster. *"Despite heavy bombardment by the Iraqi government forces, the most intense fighting has been in the Najaf and Karbala regions. The rebels have captured many towns between Basra and Baghdad."*

The newscaster continued, stating that the Kurdish rebels who claimed to hold a wide area of Iraq's rugged Northern provinces are up against Iraqi forces using surface-to-surface missiles and artillery. Five towns southeast of Karuk were now overrun by the opposition forces.

A spokesman for the Kurdish opposition said there was heavy casualties and mass destruction to their cities, forcing families to flee their homes. The Kurds were in complete control further north along the Turkish border and northeast Iran.

As the Kurds and Shiite gained control of many cities and towns, the Turkish government took a cautious step to prevent the Kurds from coming any further over the border.

Sofe turned the dial to Radio Cairo just as they announced that the unrest in Kurdistan was the subject of talks in Ankara today between the Turkish official and Foreign Minister Farook al Al Sharaa of Syria. Both Turkey and Syria, which have a large Kurdish minority, said they would be opposed to any effort by the Kurdish rebels to create their own independent state. Although the Kurds provided support for the Allied coalitions in Northern Iraq against President Hussein, the Turkish government put a great deal of pressure on the United States not to continue support the Kurds and the Shiite in the south.

The Wedding Day

The good and the bad news distracted Sofe and Almas from preparing for the wedding festivities.

Upstairs, the rest of the family were busy, with many new faces helping Shamsa and her two daughters set up outside in the courtyard.

The courtyard had a small rose garden. In front of the roses were two rows of geraniums and pansies. In between the flowers, a few herbs were planted; basal, oregano and onion. A nice patch of green grass was left in the middle that should delight those dancing. Fifteen large tables and benches were set up directly across from the buffet table where the caterer will stand.

The tables were covered with bright colored cloths. If seen from above, every three tables formed the Kurdistan flag. A bouquet of yellow flowers, resembling the sun was placed on the wedding couple's table; which was likewise draped with a white, red and green cloth. For those who wish to sit on the traditional futons and pillows for armrests, an area was arranged near the entrance of the living room.

Almas' older sister, Payman, and her husband, Faraydoon, arrived at the house after traveling a great distance from their hometown of Bitlis, about two hundred kilometers away.

Almas and Payman's mother, Golnaz, quickly walked into the living room to check on the caterer.

"Is everything okay? I just want to make sure everything will be ready."

"Don't worry, Mrs. Golnaz," the caterer, reassured, "everything is fine."

Golnaz fluttered over to Shamsa, gushing, "Oh, Shamsa, you are doing such a beautiful work decorating! The table that you have set up for the bride and groom is beautiful."

Meanwhile, Almas, Ezamalden and Delan sat comfortably on the couches in the basement listening to the radio, sipping black tea. Big smiles broke on their faces, as they heard the radio newscaster announce that the Kurds were controlling most of the Kurdish province.

In unison they let out a yell at the good news. But their celebration was halted when the newscaster added that the Republican Guard units were executing dozens of people on the streets of Basra. He quickly changed the radio dial and found an Iranian station reporting that armed Iraqi Shiite rebels are under heavy fire from Iraqi units. This including helicopter gunships carrying napalm and white phosphorous bombs.

Earlier in the week, the Syrian government quoted, Kurdish leader Jalal Talabani appealing to the United States and the coalition forces in the region, to intervene. He reportedly asked the Allies to shoot down Iraqi aircrafts that were purportedly bombing oil wells in Kirkuk.

Turning the shortwave dial again Sofe found a London spokesman for the Kurdistan Democratic Party stating that the only remaining resistance inside Kirkuk was the first Army corps. "But their morale is low", he added, "with the guerrillas attacking their barracks."

Sofe was happy with this news, but he still was frustrated that the United States would not defend the Kurds and the Shiites against Saddam's attack. Neither were a match to Saddam's powerful Air Force.

Golnaz burst into the basement, loudly chiding the boys, "Enough is enough! Haven't you heard enough? Maybe you could help us with the preparation for Almas' wedding today, since there is nothing you can do about the situation in Kurdistan or Iraq!" She started back up the stairs and stopped. They did not follow her. "If you are not coming upstairs, I will send the pigeons to scramble your radio antenna!" She continued up the stairs. They all quickly followed her out of the basement.

On his way out, Sofe shut off the radio and closed the door behind him. The men all waited for Sofe in the living room. He came upstairs, smiling, and said, "Let's have fun. Today is a very special day."Friends and relatives slowly filled up the courtyard. Freshta spotted Aziz coming through the main door, pulling a big suitcase of musical instruments. Behind him was his musician friend, Farhad, carrying his drums.

Freshta smiled shyly. "I am glad you came. We need music."

Aziz smiled back.

Noticing where his friend's attention went, Farhad walked up to the couple. Aziz suddenly noticed his friend and said, "Freshta, this is my friend Farhad, the drummer in the band."

Seeing that Aziz was entranced with this lovely lady, Farhad smiled and said to his friend, "I need to set up the speakers." Aziz replied, "I'll be right there."

Farhad disappeared from their view.

Freshta's eyes were full of bright sparks as she looked at Aziz. It was obvious they had an attraction to each other. "I guess I should help Farhad," said Aziz. Freshta nodded.

He then retrieved a clarinet and a small Kurdish drum from a suitcase and set the instruments in place. He pulled out a small box of tapes from another suitcase. He quickly and expertly hooked up the tape recorder to the receiver and tested it. He caught Freshta looking at him as he worked. And turning on the tape machine with a grin, a lively number started playing.

In no time at all, dancers lined up on the grass at the sound of the upbeat music, like a desert ground thirsty for a long-awaited rain. A young man led the dance with dynamic movements and a high energy that invited the others to follow his lead. The young man's handkerchief was tied around his neck in the colors of the Kurdish flag – yellow, red, green and white – were flying in the breeze, as he turned to the beat of the music.

Taking advantage of a good opportunity, Freshta grabbed Aziz' hand, motioning to him to dance with her. He promptly acquiesced and led her out to the grassy area with the other dancers.

The wedding celebration officially began.

A high ranking officer appeared at the door. Recognizing his good friend, Sofe greeted him. "Ali, good to see you!"

" I'm actually here on business. I don't know whether it's a good or bad day you have picked for this wedding. It *is* the Kurdish New Year, and our department is on alert. You know, there are always serious clashes with the demonstrators while people are celebrating Newroz. The New Year seems to bring out the political activism. I told the chief I wanted to stop by and make sure everything was all right here. I let him know it's Almas' wedding, so the loud music wouldn't draw suspicious attention to the department."

"Thank you, Ali. " He replied gratefully, "Can you stay for a bit"?

"I can't. Our forces are very busy today with the alert. Just enjoy your day and stay out of politics."

Just as he was about to leave Almas approached. "Congratulations on your wedding day." The conversation was interrupted when music swelled with a fast beat. Ali grinned. "This is good music!"

Then they swept Ali onto the grassy area, and joined the others, in a traditional Kurdish dance to the Turkish song.

After the dance, Ali, laughing said that he really had to go.

"Okay, okay, but not before you have some food," Sofe gestured to the tables. "Thank God you came. I feel much better that the Chief of Police knows this is only a wedding. I know the tension is high within the Turkish military forces, especially since of the Kurds and the Shiite's are controlling the borders of Northern and Southern Iraq.

Ali acknowledged his friend with a reassuring nod, then saying his farewells, Ali made for the door. Almas watched cautiously as the official left. Then drawn back to the moment by the music he turned back to the celebration.

A few hours later the music stopped and the crowd quieted as the bride arrived. Echoes of chanting started to be heard. Ronak's face was covered with bright colors of red chiffon and silk. Her father guided her towards Almas, who stood in awe at the sight of the love of his life.

Almas turned to his future father-in-law, Osman and said, "I shall respect her, love her and take care of her the rest of my life and do everything I can to make her happy. We shall have a family and keep the legacy going." He then turned to Ronak and said, "My love, I repeat to you that I will do anything within the will of God to make you happy, healthy and keep you young. And only death do us part." Ronak replied, "And I shall be a good wife to make you happy and a loving companion until death do us part."

Almas very gently removed the red silk from her face and kissed her. Everybody else came forward with hugs, kisses and "congratulations" to the bride and groom and their families.

Now, the celebration truly started. Almas asked his new bride to join him on the dance floor. They led the dance with the immediate family from both sides following them. Aziz played his favorite Kurdish dance. The chanting of joy could be heard blocks away. The rest of the wedding party joined in the dancing. Delan and Severeen, having just finished dancing, sat at a nearby table.

Delan spotted Hewa congratulating the bride and groom. Hewa then came over to Delan and Severeen and sat down. "How come you are so late?" inquired Delan. Hewa replied, "I almost didn't make it. The police attacked the people who were singing Kurdish National songs to celebrate Newroz. Then it became a demonstration and the police tried to break up the crowd, telling them to go home. But they insisted on celebrating publicly, in the street. The police started arresting people and beating them for not leaving. I had to go around and across town so I would not get too close to the demonstrators. I'm glad I made it."

"Thank God you are safe, " said Severeen.

Hearing the music, Delan, Severeen and Hewa got up from the table and started dancing. Slowly, the entire family joined the excitement of dancing. Delan could see Sofe smiling, having a great time.

After a few more dances, the bride and groom cut the cake. And everyone enjoyed the desert and tea. Then, all too soon the sun was setting, and the festivities wound down.

As the tired, but happy guests began their goodbyes and the caterer and his crew started the clean up, Hewa, Delan and Severeen, sat discussing their plan to cross the Iraqi border. "Even though we are traveling legally with all our passports and documents, our problem is the Turkish military, stationed on the border." Hewa remarked. "I understand there are hundreds of thousands of Turkish soldiers put on alert on this side of the border. But we have still have to be very careful because of the tension and of the Kurds into Turkey."

Delan leaned closer, "We are going with Ezamalden the day after tomorrow to Snura, which is a few miles from the border. Ezamalden's son-in-law, Mahdy, lives in Zakhu. He drives a taxi between Iraq and Turkey. Ezamalden told me that he knows almost all of the Border Patrol, on both sides of the checkpoint. Ezamalden is going to talk to him about taking us across the border."

***

The Wedding Day

Two days later, March 23, 1991, Ezamalden and his family were in Mahdy's white taxi, leading a second taxi carrying Delan, Severeen and Hewa. Frequently, they had stopped at inspection checkpoints along the way. By the end of the day they arrived at Snura; a little town nestled along the side of a beautiful, snowcapped mountain. Most of the homes are carved out of the hillside, all built out of adobe bricks.

They arrived at the home of Ezamalden. He had a two story house, with three bedrooms on the top floor. On the second floor was a living room and a large kitchen that were practically carved out of the mountain with the staircase coming down to the courtyard. There was a stable directly under the bedrooms with a big door open to the courtyard for the livestock.

After getting out of the taxis, they all made their way through the cattle and goats, and climbed the outdoor staircase to the living room.. They were greeted by one of Shamsa's relatives who house sits for them when they are out of town. In the living room there were many comfortable futons on the floor against the wall and a fire drum in the middle of the room for heating. They always kept a large, black kettle full of water on the top of the metal fireplace.

They were all sitting around the fireplace, talking, while Shamsa and her daughter, Shanaz, prepared some food for dinner. Delan pulled his sketchbook from his backpack. With his artistic eye, he watched Severeen and sketched her when she was not aware.

Suddenly Salman, Shamsa's precocious seven-year old son, said, "Draw me first!" and he posed with a smile in front of Severeen. A few minutes later Delan lifted his pencil from the sketchpad and the boy inched closer for a look.

"That's me!," he beamed with delight. "Did you learn this in school?"

"Yes," Delan nodded. "We had arts classes in high school that made me want go to the Fine Art Institute to really learn artwork. We used to go on field trips where I did a lot of landscapes. We also had models to pose for us in school. I always loved art."

Shevan stared at Delan admiringly, "When I grow up I want to be like you. I want to be an artist."

"Who is going to teach you?" asked Salman, "Most of the time we don't even have a regular teacher."

"We had two teachers. But not too long ago they took one away and they have not replaced him," Salman offered sadly.

"Who took him away?" asked Delan.

"The Secret Police", answered Salman, "They said he was sympathetic to the PKK. All he did was complain about the condition of the school. We don't even have enough desks and chairs to sit on it. Most of the time two or three students have to share one book and take turns taking it home for study. He wanted to improve all these conditions so they fired him. Students come from far away because this is the only school in this area we have to shut up and not complain about anything. We had no electricity, and no running water so when the young people grew up, they couldn't wait to leave this village because there's nothing for them to do."

"I am sorry about all this, said Delan sympathetically, "Maybe some day I will come and teach the arts here."

Hewa started laughing.

"Dinner is ready!" Shamsa announced.

As they sat on the futons around a big copper tray, reminiscent of a round table without legs, Shamsa brought out the delicious dinner of onion stew and chicken, with sawar, a rice-like cracked wheat dish. There was a silence as the hungry guests served themselves. But just as they had filled their plates and ready to feast -- off in the distance, there was the sudden distinct *'rat-tat-tat'* of a machine gun.

"We have become used to that sound," Ezamalden reassured her startled guests, "It is one of the main problems we have here in Snura because we are right on the border of Iraq and Turkey. Sometimes it gets very bad, and we hear from our neighbors the next day about who was injured or killed, and how many people were arrested." Pausing, she nonchalantly took a bite of food and shrugged her shoulders.

"It's becoming our way of life and everyone prays that they won't be a victim, caught in the crossfire. It's no way to live, but what can we do?"

Staring at the host, in a daze, Severeen and Delan shook their heads in agreement.

***

The next morning, after breakfast, Delan was very anxious to cross the border. It was close to noon when Mahdy, Ezamalden's son-in-law, showed up in his taxi. He greeted his passengers and started loading his taxi with their suitcases and backpacks.

"Can I see your passports?" he asked as the trio entered the vehicle. "We don't want any problems. You don't know how picky the border patrol can be." Farewells were exchanged. Ezamalden, his family, Shevan and Salman were sad to see them go.

"We will come back to visit with you on our way back", Delan promised the boys. He gave them each a reassuring hug before he entered the car. They all waved their hands out of the taxi until they disappeared around the bend.

At the border checkpoint two stern-looking patrol agents waited. One peered into the car, then looked at their passports for the appropriate stamps, while the other scrutinized Delan's papers.

"This is a French passport, yet you are from Iraq?"

"Yes."

The agents then silently switched places and repeated the process.

As a nervous Mahdy casually chatted with the authorities, the vehicle and each passenger's bags were searched thoroughly, item by item. Then, after the group was grossly overcharged for the necessary passport stamps, the bags were re-tied on top of the taxi.

Next stop, the Iraqi checkpoint.

There everything went smoothly and quickly. As they were leaving, one of the Kurdish officers looked at Delan and said, "I'm surprised you're coming into Iraq. You do know that thousands of people are leaving?"

"I know," answered cautiously Delan, "but we have to go."

"I wish you all good luck," the Kurdish soldier saluted.

After a short ride, they arrived at Zakhu. It was late in the afternoon and they were all very hungry. They asked Mahdy where they should go for a late lunch. "I know just the place!"

At the restaurant they were greeted by Abbas, the owner, who embraced Mahdy. "My good friends here, are very hungry!"

"Mahdy's friends are always welcome!" Abbas smiled, leaning close to Mahdy, "Where are you taking them?"

"Sulaymaniyah."

"Oh!" he turned to Delan," Just minutes ago I heard on the radio reported that Saddam was bombing the big cities in Kurdistan from the air. I hope it's not true."

"I thought the U.S. and the Allied forces didn't allow Saddam Hussein to fly helicopter gunships and fixed wing jets, " said Delan.

"They let the Iraqi fighter bombers and helicopter gunships bomb the area around the city of Kirkuk. They raided it early Monday morning causing heavy casualties, according to the radio broadcast from Iran which was monitored by the BBC." He continued to say that the Kurdish resistance, Peshmerga claimed they shot down one helicopter.

"The radio announced that Kurdistan is under the control of the Kurds." Abbas continued, " but the Iraqi Army is gaining control. I am listening mainly to the Tehran station on my shortwave radio. I am sorry that you have a long journey ahead of you. I wish you the best of luck."

Abbas excused himself and walked over to some of his other customers, making sure everything was all right. Delan and Severeen gazed silently at Hewa, worried expression.

Moments later, Abbas returned to their table with menus and more news. "According to Tehran radio, troops from the Republican guards attacked demonstrators opposed to Hussein with phosphorous, napalm bomb and poison gas grenades."

Bending to set a bottle of wine on the table, his voice lowered, "Someone from the Shiite group rebels in Damascus estimated that more than 20,000 people had been killed in fighting with Iraqi soldiers, just 3-1/2 hours since the golf war ended. Saddam appears to have concentrated most of his efforts on breaking the back of the rebels in the South, and making little attempt on Kurds in Kurdistan. " Abbas, raised himself back to his full height. "But, you know, none of this can be verified."

Hewa looked at Mahdy with concern. "We will go as far as we can. I just hope there is no problem."

Delan looked around the restaurant, his eyes looking everywhere. "Why I didn't buy one in France. It would have been much cheaper."

"Buy?," Hewa asked.

"A short-wave radio."

"Not to worry, they sell them cheap here. Almost everyone has a radio in this town. It's our connection to the outside world," said Mahdy.

Abbas laughed, "Yes. Just a block away, on the right side of the street; Kandeel Electronics. The owner is my brother, Hamdi. Tell him I sent you. He'll give you a good deal."

After a filling meal the travellers thanked Abbas for his hospitality and the latest headlines, then started up the street.

Walking through the crowds of shoppers, who seemed oblivious to chaos of the surrounding world, Mahdy quickly found the electronics store and motioned his friends to follow him inside.

"Excuse me, is your name Hamdi?"

"Yes, it is. What can I do for you?"

"Your brother, Abbas, sent us. We are looking for a shortwave radio."

"I have been selling a lot of them lately. Everybody wants to know what's going on in Iraq. From day to day it's a different story, unfortunately. I have a small, short-wave radio that has great reception – even better than the larger one." Retrieving the receiver from the shelf, he continued, "It even has a fine tuner that brings in every station very clearly."

Mahdy and Delan studied the device, noting the dial was displayed in both Arabic and English. And after turning the dial to a few clear stations, twenty-five U.S. dollars was laid on the counter in exchange.

On the sidewalk, Delan handed Severeen their new purchase. "Now we are ready to travel."

Hewa interrupted the couple when he remarked, "So let's talk about our route to Sulayman," Hewa advised.

"What do you suggest we do?" Delan's expression turned serious.

"Let's stay here in Zakhu. We will get a hotel for a few days. We can access the situation and plan our routes accordingly.

Confiding that his home in Zakhu, was to small to put up everyone up. Mahdy added that he had a friend who owned hotel with a hot shower and a small kitchen. Severeen perked up at this news, but added shyly, "We will need two rooms."

Delan was hesitant about this idea. "Maybe we should press onward."

Mahdy reminded him that they already spent a couple of weeks in Diyarbakir and that a few more days in Zakhu would not make a difference at this point. He continued, "We can listen to your radio, and see when it would be safer to travel."

"My brother is expecting us in Sulaymaniyah," replied Delan. "But I'm sure he will hear what is going on and figure we were not safe to travel there to meet him yet. He would hopefully come here to Zakhu."

Mahdy excused himself to use the public telephone. A few minutes later, he returned smiling.

"I got you guys two rooms! One has a kitchen. He can't hold them for long. We need to move quickly. With all the trouble here, they will go fast."

They were able to forget their problems for a while and found themselves enjoying their stay as they explored the city of Zakhu.

Zakhu

On Thursday, March 28, 1991, Delan came out of his room, jumping for joy. He looked around, only to see Severeen sitting outside in the garden of the hotel, which overlooked the whole city. "I just heard on the radio that yesterday the Kurdish rebel leaders captured two Soviet made planes and took over an Iraqi air base. They also seized a government camp on the road between Dohuk to Mosul. The air base and the camp were among the last posts under government control in Northern Iraq."

As he concluded Hewa appeared with a big smile, "Guess what I just heard on the radio?"

"Please, tell us," Severeen coaxed

"A group of South Korean and Bangladesh workers from the major oil center of Kirkuk said that all the villages they passed through in the last three days were in the hands of rebel Kurds!"

Delan found a radio station reporting the rest of the story. The leader of patriotic Union of Kurdistan said that near the Turkish border, a Mig 21 fighter plane and a Sukhoi bomber were both seized, still intact, even though the government destroyed three other planes before fleeing. The London broadcast further reported that the Kurdish Democratic Party stated that the attack on the Khalid Air Base was launched to stop the bombing of the rebel held area that the Kurds now controlled in the North. There were also reports of Iraqi success in squashing the rebellion in the South by Shiite Muslims, who were also trying to overthrow Hussein's regime. The official Iraqi press quoted the government as saying that "peace, stability and order had returned to Southern Iraq."

Little hope was given to all those rebels who were attempting to force Hussein out of power.

The excitement of these new developments left the listeners emotionally drained. Severeen finally turned the radio off with a sigh, "We will do what we have to do, one day at a time."

In spite of the roller-coaster feeling of not having any control of their destiny, Mahdy, Delan and Severeen all agreed they should continue their journey to Sulaymaniyah.

Listening to the radio all day in the car, Severeen had a bad feeling about spending the night in Mosul. "We should stop until we know it is safe."

Mahdy agreed, especially after noticing the increasing traffic heading the opposite direction from them, going north towards the border. "Something must have happened in the last 24 hours that we haven't heard about yet," Mahdy feared. "And I' don't think I want to know."

They drove into the small town of Tal-Kayf and found a hotel. In the lobby they overheard a Kurdish family talking about the bombing in Kirkuk by Hussein's military forces. Delan was very upset by this news and approached to the patriarch of the family, "Excuse me, I could not help but overhear what you were saying. We are on our way to Kirkuk, then to Sulaymaniyah."

"My friend," said the old man, tearfully, "Sulaymaniyah could be hit worse than Kirkuk. There is tragedy everywhere. Though we escaped, I don't know where to go. Like most of families from there, we don't have passports. We are just running.

"Saddam's forces came back to Kirkuk, first by air attacks, then by land, destroying buildings and homes with bulldozers, killing thousands of people. The Kurdish resistance could not hold on."

The man lowered his head, sadly, looking at the ground with an expression of defeat. The tears overflowed. "We were lucky to get out in time before they bulldozed our house – right in front of our eyes!"

Delan took his radio from his pocket, found a Cairo channel and the two listened.

The Kurdish rebels were rushing to Kirkuk to confront the assault by the 150,000 Iraqi forces who attacked and captured the city the night before. Pro-Iranian Shiite Muslims rose up in the South, Iraqi forces had literally taken over all the towns in Southern Iraq.

The Bush Administration concluded that a rebel overthrow of Hussein would lead to the disintegration of Iraq, so the United States continued to permit Hussein to use helicopter gunships to fight the rebel forces throughout Iraq. The radio commentator from Cairo objected to what the U.S. was allowing, stating that it goes against the principles of America, which supposedly believes in freedom and self-determination of all peoples.

The Kurdish man looked at Delan and said, "Don't go to Sulaymaniyah. Please. It's probably under Iraqi control now. They will kill you. Go back to the border, to Zakhu, and try to get out of Iraq as soon as possible. You will have a better chance. If they catch us, they will send us to a camp, near the Turkish border. We are so tired of running. We have no hope."

Delan thanked him for his time, and wished him and his family well.

As the old man and his family walked away, Delan turned back to Mahdy and Hewa, "I'm going back to Zakhu and I hope you do the same. We can monitor the situation for a few days. It would be safer than being here."

Mahdy agreed, "This would be the wisest thing to do right now.

A half a block away from the hotel, Mahdy stopped to get some sodas when the sound of helicopters suddenly passed over head. An instant later an explosion erupted just beyond the hotel. The pedestrians scurried off in every direction, screaming. In the confusion another helicopter appeared, blasting a rocket directly through the hotel foyer.

Delan and Severeen looked at each other and bolted towards the hotel. Entering through the hole where the door had been, they carefully stepped into the smoked-filled building, negotiating their way through the debris and body parts. Before them were the lifeless bodies of the Kurdish family, who Delan had just talked to minutes earlier.

Suddenly Mahdy appeared through the smoke, grabbing at their sleeves with both hands, ushering Severeen and Delan out to their waiting car, "No time! We have to get out of here. Hurry!"

Severeen's tears were out of control watching, through the speeding car's back window, as the devastating scene faded into the smoke.

The northbound highway to Zakhu was congested with automobiles, trucks and tractors. The southbound lane was likewise full with families traveling by foot, all walking north, towards the border.

Upon arriving in Zakhu later that day, Mahdy drove straight to the hotel, where a long line of people waited to get in. Mahdy quickly got out of his taxi with Delan and Hewa right behind him. Once inside, they moved through the crowd up to the front desk. Mahdy asked, "Do you have any rooms available?"

"Sorry, sir, no vacancies since yesterday."

They got back into the car and drove by the other hotels. It was the same everywhere – no vacancy. Mahdy finally stopped the car. "No sense wasting gas. I am taking you to my house. It's very humble and small, but I have one extra bedroom."

Delan glanced at Severeen, who was very tired at this point, "We are very thankful. We will pay you for it."

"You pay for the car expenses because that's how I make my living, but you are my guests in my house and it would be an insult to me if you paid to be a guest in my home" Mahdy countered.

"We really appreciate your hospitality, Mahdy," Hewa nodded gratefully.

***

Saddam Hussein ordered the Iraqi military forces to bomb all the cities in Kurdistan. For two continuous days, Delan, Severeen, Hewa and Mahdy stood at the Iraqi border, watching what seemed to be a million people fleeing from Iraq into Turkey; traveling down the only road between the two countries. And as they watched, Delan prayed that his brother, Rebwar, was among them.

The American troops, stationed throughout the southern Iraqi cities and towns, were under strict orders of the Bush Administration to not interfere in the uprising. Helplessly, they watched the Republican Guard brutally massacre civilian men, women and children, and even shell hospital and refugee camps.

The green flag of the Shiite Resistance fell from communication towers. They could not fight the opposition's tanks and artillery with mere rifles.

Delan dialed his shortwave set to Radio Tehran, just as in time to hear an American G.I., Captain Miller, say how frustrated he was with the U.S. foreign policy. "My buddies and I would go north and enter Baghdad, if we could! We would be glad to take Saddam Hussein down. We are ready!"

More than two thousand refugees and resistance fighters soon flooded the United States-held refinery on the city's outskirts, in the southern part of Iraq. Men and boys over the age of twelve were being executed and buried in mass graves. Black clad women and crying children camped in a few still-standing buildings and drank from pool water, covered with thick algae. One ten-year-old had lost his hand and another child had been machine-gunned. An eighteen-month old child miraculously survived being shot in the chest at point blank range with a pistol.

"When someone brings you a small baby with powder burns on his chest what can you say?," an American solider asked, shaking his head. "What kind of people would do this?"

On the concrete floor of a bombed-out oil tank, a 52 year old man, well dressed survivor suddenly appeared to plea for assistance in broken English. The soldier apologetically explained that they could not help. The man began to cry. He then tore up a handful of Iraqi dinars, stomped on the remains and spat furiously on the ground. "The world does not care," he lamented in Arabic, "We are carrying the burden of the crime of one man!" he before he disappeared." Hewa shook his head and said, "This is a tragedy and it's getting out of control."

In the middle of this, Hewa laid a reassuring hand on Delan's shoulder, "Your brother knows you're here. I'm quite sure you will find each other. But," he turned to the others apologetically, "I really have to get back to Turkey, and then on to France. You should think about leaving here. Come back when it's not so dangerous."

"No," Delan shook his head with determination. "We will go on to the refugee camp tomorrow. I just hope we can find people from Sulaymaniyah."

The next day Delan and Severeen heard the echo machine guns in the distance. Not knowing whether Saddam would do to Zakhu, Delan switched on the shortwave for the news from Cairo, Tehran and Nicosia.

Radio Tehran reported that tens of thousands of family refugees were under the crossfire of fighting in Iraq and were waiting processing at the refugee camps set up in Semdinili and Curkurka. It was suddenly announced that the border was closed because they could not permit the mass entry of Iraqi Kurds fleeing Saddam's military forces. Hearing the news Severeen and Delan tearfully retreated to their room, placing their suitcase in front of the door. Severeen put her hand between Delan's shoulder blades and rubbed very gently until he turned around. Silently they looked into each other's eyes, reclined together on the bed and embraced.

They woke up the next day, with Mahdy gently knocking on their door. "Severeen, Delan," he whispered, "Are you all right?" Delan jumped up bed and opened the door:

"Mahdy. Did Hewa get the taxi to Diyarbakir?"

"He is probably there by now. I'm sorry that your trip to Sulaymaniyah is not possible. Listen to the news. It's pretty bad everywhere in Kurdistan. But there is good news," Mahdy forced smile, "Selma made breakfast."

Delan breathed a sigh. "You two have been so kind. We appreciate your hospitality."

"I'm so hungry, I could eat a pig!." Severeen added, leaning her head on Delan's arm.

"Oh, no, we don't eat pigs!" Mahdy cautioned. "Sometimes we hunt them and give them to our Assyrian Christian neighbors…You're Christian?"

She nodded with a hungry, "Yes."

"If you want to wait a few days, we will hunt down one for you," Mahdy chuckled, "there are more pigs here than Christians."

Instead, Delan and Severeen were offered the promise of scrambled eggs, which Mahdy called, 'kuckoo'. "Don't ask me why," he explained. "It was my father's favorite breakfast."

"No more joking about food," Selma playfully scolded, cracking another egg over the skillet. "Be thankful we have chickens. There are shortages everywhere; food, shelter, sanitized drinking water. Saddam's forces are taking control here in Zakhu. Stores and restaurants are closing. The refugee camp is becoming so big, there must be 50,000 waiting to cross. People are leaving in droves for the border." Placing a large platter of 'kuckoo' on the table, she added, "I hope you two will be safe."

As Severeen helped Selma clean up after their breakfast, Delan and Mahdy listened to British broadcaster Tom Carver described countless painful scenes of ill-fed and poorly-clothed people struggling to escape.

People, young and old and not in such good health were reportedly taking up to two days to get to the border. They trekked along snow covered ridges of the mountains. Some of the children had no shoes. They would stand in the snowy field crying because their feet were frozen.

Over fifty thousand Kurds struggled across passes near the southeastern border town of Uludere in Turkey. Turkey's hardline stand against a mass migration was created because of the lingering resentment over the international response to the sudden flood of 60,000 Iraqi Kurds. These Kurds fled into Turkey in the late summer of 1988 and accused Hussein's troops of attacking their villages with chemical weapons. At that time Iraq agreed to a creasefire in its eight year war against Iran.

***

Hearing this news, Delan announced, "Severeen and I will go to the refugee camp nearby to see if anybody came from Sulaymaniyah."

"Why are you going there?" Mahdy questioned. "Your brother would probably come here, to Zakhu, to look for you before he would go to the refugee camp."

"I wouldn't mind going in there. I could volunteer my nursing skills." Severeen, interrupted, gazing at Delan with devotion.

Outvoted, Mahdy sighed, "It's only a few kilometers from here. I'll drive you."

The Camp

As they travelled towards the mountains, their car shared the road with a seemingly endless caravan of refugees. It was a long, winding, human trail of disappointed men, women and children.

Still a distance from the mountain camp, Mahdy stopped the car. Severeen and Delan stepped out with their little backpacks, and after their "goodbyes," they blended into the slow cadence of the dreary parade.

After what seemed an agonizing forever, a Red Cross tent appeared in the distance. On closer inspection, the couple witnessed yet another long line; this one comprised of the sick and hungry enduring the endless wait for treatment.

Entering the tent the two introduced themselves. And Severeen immediately offered the overworked staff her nursing skills.

The doctor in charge looked at her ID and passport and smiled in relief. "I am Dr. Gerard and you are indeed welcome."

"Ahh, French?," Severeen inquired.

"Oui," the doctor nodded, "from Paris."

"Me, as well."

Aware of the many patience waiting, Delan gave a warm hug to Severeen a warm hug, "I'll be back in a few hours."

To pass the time Delan found a large piece of cardboard, pulled a few sharpened art pencils he kept in his bag and began to spell out phrase using large letters: *"Looking for my brother, Rebwar, from Sulaymaniyah."*

It wasn't long before the sign caught the eye of a passerby. "Most of the people from Sulaymaniyah ran towards Iranian border," the man volunteered, pointing over the mountains. "I don't think you'll find your brother here."

Delan thanked him, but he knew his brother would come.

He continued walking, giving most of his bottled water to thirsty children. Then he found a man from Sulaymaniyah, who was visiting relatives in Kirkuk when the Iraqi forces attacked them. "Without knowing what direction I was going, I ended up here." Delan told the stranger of his brother's intentions; about how his brother was supposed to meet him.

"I don't think he will come from Kirkuk," the man advised, "He will have to travel a roundabout route through Irbil to Agra, then Dahuk, to arrive in Zakhu. I wish you good luck finding him."

After a few hours, Delan returned to the Red Cross tent. Standing just inside the opening, he watched Severeen assist the other nurses. Admiring her skill and dedication, he marveled as she tended to both a sick child, and the baby's equally ill and uncooperative parents.

Excusing herself from the family Severeen walked over to Delan.

"Dr. Gerard asked me if I could work for a few days."

Seeing that she really wanted to help here, Delan whispered, "Where would we stay?"

"We would share the tent with them." She snuggled into Delan. "It will only be a couple nights."

"I can see you are needed here. I wish I could be more helpful."

"You are being helpful by being so patient with me." Severeen smiled, kissing his cheek.

"This will also give us a few more days to wait for my brother. Hopefully, by then most of the refugees will have crossed the border."

Severeen went back to work and Delan walked back out into the camp. He took out his pad of paper and pencils and started to sketch. He realized it was much easier when he used to have models. The real tragedy here was much harder to observe.

As an artist, Delan felt compelled more than ever to draw the reality set before his eyes. Though at times, the sights he witnessed were horrific he pushed himself and his pencil to continue; for in some strange way he sensed that his artwork would ultimately be a service to mankind.

After finishing one piece, he noticed a beautiful woman holding her child. For a few moments he gazed at this mother and child. Then the horror of what he saw came into focus: neither the child nor the mother moved.

A woman stopped next to Delan and whispered, "Her child died yesterday, but she will not let the baby go. She has said nothing. She just sits there, frozen in time; in total shock. And there's nothing we could do."

Delan was putting the finishing touches on the drawing when Severeen appeared by his side. "That's a very nice drawing." Looking up at her with tears in his eyes, he told Severeen the story. "She really needs help."

Cautiously the young nurse approached the mother so as not to alarm her. She touched the baby's wrist for a pulse. The mother suddenly fell to the ground, unconscious.

Delan ran to the tent to get help, while Severeen tried to revive her. Moments later, Dr. Gerard came running, just when two Kurdish man carried her lifeless body toward them. The mother had died and there was nothing anyone could do for her.

The same woman who spoke to Delan earlier told the doctor that the poor woman's husband and son were killed right in front of her eyes by a machine gun on a helicopter gunship five days prior.

"We tried then to help her, but we could not communicate with her. Then her baby was killed.

We have all lost loved ones. I lost my dear husband last week. None of us know from day to day what is going to happen," the woman lamented.

Across from the camp on a small hill, they buried the mother and child. They must have dug at least ten other new graves that day.

"We have a very limited supply of medicine," Dr. Gerard confessed. "Many of those with severe injuries die because we can't do anything for them, and many of them die of hunger and freezing cold. No one expected this exodus." He turned to Severeen, "I hope you have a better chance of surviving on the other side of the border. There must be at least 100,000 people there by now, and that number is increasing every day."

Delan switched his radio on just in time to hear President Ozal of Turkey acknowledge that his country, "risks being overwhelmed by the flood of refugees fleeing from Saddam's forces."

"I think everybody who fought to liberate Kuwait should help the Kurds," Dr. Gerard professed, showing his irritation. "When Iraq's powerful modern army wages high-tech war against overmatched Kurdish guerrilla forces, they kill and uproot innocent civilian populations, which verges on genocide.

"What should Americans think when Turkish forces attack the Kurds in Southeastern Turkey? Or when Turkish planes bomb an Iraqi Kurdish area, as they have at least five times in the past few months? The American response has of course been muted, since Turkey has a democratically elected government. It is a NATO ally and a valued member of the coalition against Saddam Hussein. Turkey faces an armed Kurdish guerrilla movement operating out of sanctuaries in Iraq and Syria. None of this justifies ugly repression against Kurdish civilians in Turkey, as they did in Iraq. The Kurdish people desperately need the international community to demand restraint."

Venting his frustration, the doctor continued. "The large Kurdish population in Turkey has fared better by comparison, but its situation is deteriorating rapidly. The Kurds in Turkey have been subject to systematic human rights violations, including torture. In addition they are caught between military and guerrilla fire. In both countries, the Kurds are in acute danger. The international community is not required to support the separatist demand for Kurdish state. But it's normally bound to demand that both Baghdad and Ankara cease their ugly repression of Kurdish civilians, before it becomes a genocide," Dr. Gerard concluded with great emotion.

Delan studied the doctor for a moment then asked, "What brought you here, to the Kurdish cause?"

"I volunteer wherever a disaster or situation like this takes place. I am not married. I have no home, at least for now. My 'family' is all of humanity in need. This situation, here, happened very quickly and unexpectedly. Good thing I had two assistants to help me, and of course, Severeen."

Dr. Gerard noticed Delan's drawings peeking out of his backpack. "May I see them?"

Delan carefully extracted the sketches and handed them to the doctor, one by one.

"These are very good. You picked very good subjects." Stopping briefly at the sketch of the mother and her lifeless baby, Gerard exhaled, "These images are moving."

Slowly leafing through them, he whispered, "The way you handle the pencil lines...the way you put pressure on your pencil to create a depth and shadow...you must have studied the masters quite a bit."

"You are quite knowledgeable about art," Delan likewise observed, "I've always loved the compositions of the greats; Raphael, DaVinci, and Durer, the German artist. They were the true masters!"

Dr. Gerard nodded in appreciation, "I quite agree. I took some art classes in college while I studying medicine. I hope that, like the masters, these works of yours will one day be seen by the world --displayed in a proper gallery."

Emotional Exploration

By the third day, the medical team's work had slowed down as most of the refugees crossed the border, thus allowing Delan to visit his indispensable companion.

Seeing the way the two looked at each other, Dr. Gerard winked at Severeen. "Why don't you take Delan for a walk in the hills. It's a beautiful day." Smiling at the suggestion, she took Delan's hand and motioned him to follow.

As they walked out of the camp into a meadow covered with narcissus, Severeen and Delan could see the melting snow on the distant mountains. Departing momentarily from the human imperfection, the happy couple silently took in the simple and unselfish side of nature. It was a true Spring day.

Opening her backpack Severeen pulled out a small blanket. Laying on it, Delan did likewise, reclining next to her. They were completely overwhelmed by the beauty of nature. Facing each other, they gazed into the other's eyes, communicating without words. And there, just over the hill from the horrors of war, the two embraced, finally experience the full depth of love without boundaries. Realizing how much they had missed before this moment, they explored each other's inner souls. But even as their bodies intertwined they remained aware of their chaotic surroundings.

Holding Delan tightly, Severeen exhaled, "I could not imagine life or love without you."

Delan kissed her sweetly. "Nothing seems right in this world, but you and this moment."

After a swirl of bliss and satisfaction, Severeen shivered in the sudden cold. Both time and the sun had shifted. "It's getting late, I guess we should go." Neither of them moved, not wanting the moment to end.

Eventually Severeen folded little blanket and put it away in her backpack. Delan splashed his face with the cold water from a nearby stream. And turning into the meadow he walked among the Narcissus, picking a handful, smelling each one with delight.

Severeen watched admiringly as he approached her with his colorful bouquet. With a playful, curtsied bow she accepted his aromatic gift. "For the most beautiful woman in my life."

After a lingering kiss, the two walked slowly around the bend and re-entered the world.

***

In front of the Red Cross tent they looked at each other and expressed feelings of contentment and satisfaction. It was now time to go back to work and turn the chapter back to the painful reality of what man brings upon himself.

Around noon the next day, Severeen came out of the tent to see Delan waiting for her; he was sketching a few people who were in the process of crossing the border. "That is so beautiful, Delan", Severeen said, admiring his work. Suddenly, they both looked up when they heard the blare of an automobile horn. It looked like Mahdy's white taxi. And when it got closer, they saw it was, indeed, Mahdy in the driver's seat. He stopped right in front of them. Happy to see his friends, he beamed.

"I hope you didn't think I forgot you. I knew you were busy here. But hearing that most of the refugees have crossed the border, I figured you should not stay here much longer. Zakhu is not safe anymore! Saddam's forces are all over the town."

After quickly grabbing their backpacks, the couple returned to the tent where Severeen gave Dr. Gerard a farewell kiss and her sister's Paris telephone number. Though sad, the Red Cross team thanked the two for all their help and offered them a wave as the taxi doors closed.

At Mahdy's house, Delan went to pick up their luggage; he pulled out some cash and thrust it into the taxi driver's hand. Mahdy tried to refuse the money, but Delan insisted, "Remember, that's how you make your living."

"Thank you," Mahdy nodded, "It has been a pleasure knowing you both." And without looking, he reluctantly tucked the folded currency into his pocket.

Delan and Severeen hugged Selma, and thanked her for all her kindness and generosity. "We will never forget you two."

Be safe!"

But both couples knew that there was little chance of that.

Rebwar

A young, slim, good-looking man with dark complexion stepped ahead in a line of travellers waiting to register at a hotel's busy front desk. "Have you by chance seen a man named Delan and his fiancée, Severeen? They might have stayed here a few days ago."

The manager checked his book. "I don't see those names. I am sorry."

Undaunted, the young man left and walked to the next hotel, where he asked the same question. Shaking his head 'No', the clerk suggested another hotel a few blocks away.

At the next registration desk, he arrived just as the inn keeper was announcing, "No more rooms."

Pushing passed the disappointed crowd he called out, "Please. I just have a question. I'm looking for a young man, Delan and his fiancée, Severeen. She is French."

"Those names are not in the book. And I would remember a French girl," he smiled. "In case they come in, who should I say is asking for them?"

"Tell them, Rebwar was here."

"How many hotels have you tried?"

"The two down the street," he pointed wearily.

"There are only five hotels in this area. You should try the Serwan Hotel, just outside of town. Its too far to walk. Take a taxi. The driver will know how to get there."

Rebwar thanked the manager for the information, and quickly hailed a taxi outside.

"Serwan Hotel?" the driver repeated, "Don't waste your time. They haven't had a vacancy for the last two days."

"I am actually looking for my brother and I think he stayed in one of these hotels," said Rebwar.

Pulling up to the Serwan, the driver sighed, "Good luck. With all the refugees coming through here, you will need it."

At the front desk Rebwar was met by a familiar scene; a line of weary travellers, a placard announcing "NO VACANCY" and an exasperated clerk constantly repeating the phrase, "Can't you people read the sign?"

Despite this swirl of confusion, Rebwar, leaned across the desk and attempted to get the clerk's attention. But before he could speak, the man behind the counter glanced at him with a look of recognition. "You look familiar," the clerk pointed to Rebwar, "Have you been here before?"

Hope wash over the young man. "No, I have not, but I am looking for my brother and we look very much alike. Have you by chance seen him? He is with his fiancée, Severeen.

"Oh, my goodness. So, *you* are Delan's brother!"

Rebwar's eyes opened with excitement and he could not control the smile. 'Please, where are they?" he asked.

"They were in town last week and they stayed here one night before they left to go to the South. You know, unfortunately, how the situation is. They returned here to Zakhu the very next day. I didn't have a vacancy for them, so I believe they stayed at a friend's house."

"Did they mention who they might be staying with?"

"His name is Mahdy, a taxi driver who comes by here to drop off hotel guests."

"How I can I reach him?"

Shaking his head, the clerk sadly, "I've talked to him so many times. I should know him better. Maybe you should ask the other taxi drivers around town. Hopefully, one of them will know where you can find him."

Disappointed but still undaunted Rebwar found the line of taxi drivers parked along the sidewalk near the hotel. He asked them, one by one, if they knew Mahdy. They all declined knowing him personally.

Then it dawned on the young man that the drivers probably knew Mahdy very well, but were silent out caution.

"What if this stranger before them was a member of Saddam's Baath Party?" Rebwar considered, "Giving unsolicited information could mean death them - or Mahdy. Especially now that Saddam's forces were slowly coming back and taking control of the town."

Still, Rebwar kept asking more taxi drivers.

A few blocks away, he saw a taxi driver in the distance, who was leaning on the fender of his car, looking bored for lack of business. He walked very quickly towards the taxi driver. The taxi driver perked up when he noticed Rebwar heading in his direction. Maybe this was his next customer! Rebwar came up to him and inquired if he knew a taxi driver named Mahdy.

"He is a friend of my brother and I understand he may know his whereabouts." Not giving the man time to speak, and with such desperation, Rebwar continued, "My brother and I are from Halabja. I was living and going to school in Sweden, and when I heard about Saddam Hussein's chemical bomb attacks, I came home to Halabja to find that most of my family were dead. I found out my brother, Delan, was still alive and was taken to France for medical help. I then heard word that he was trying to return home from Zakhu. He was stopped in route when the Kurds and Shiite failed to overthrow Saddam. I had to detour through the back roads of Sulaymaniyah, to get here, to Zakhu, hoping to find my brother."

Rebwar could not say another word. He simply looked at the stranger in front of him, spent.

The taxi driver was intoxicated by all this personal information he received from Rebwar. He felt sad. But still, he asked Rebwar, "Can you prove your identification as you claim?" Rebwar immediately pulled out his Swedish identification.

The taxi driver was really affected by what Rebwar said. He replied, "I'm sorry about what you have gone through. My name is Majeed. Mahdy is a very good friend of mine and I will take you to where he lives. I have not seen him for awhile because he's been so busy lately taking passengers across the border to Diyarbakir in Turkey.

Majeed opened the door of his taxi. Rebwar excitedly jumped in with his small duffel bag.

"You don't know how much I appreciate this. I have not seen my brother in years, " Rebwar tearfully said.

"Mahdy is a very nice man and his wife, Selma, is very close to my wife. I am going to take you to Mahdy's house. We can see if he ever met your brother. He might not be home right now, but Selma may know something. She is from Kurdistan, right across from the Turkish border, so Mahdy prefers to work between the two countries. Quite often when it's late, he just stays at his in-laws in a small village called Snura. When he does go all the way to Diyarbakir, he will stay overnight, across the border with his relatives, instead of driving back the 250 kilometers to home.   I just hope he's not there now."

Majeed stopped in front of Mahdy's house. He jumped out of his car, ahead of Rebwar, and ran up onto the porch of the small, one-story house and knocked on the door.

Mahdy's wife, Selma, opened the door and with surprise, exclaimed, " Majeed, how nice to see you! It's been a long time." Rebwar came closer into view. Selma took a second look at him and with instant recognition said, "You must be Delan's brother! You look just like him!" This made Rebwar very happy.

"I am Mahdy's wife, Selma."

Majeed excused himself, saying he had to get back to work. Rebwar attempted to pay him for the ride and his time, but Majeed refused. Rebwar reluctantly put his money away and thanked him for all his help. He turned toward Selma and entered the house.

Selma closed the door and then she listened to Rebwar explain his plight. In a sympathetic manner, she suggested, "When Mahdy gets back, we will see what he knows." Rebwar thanked her and continued to tell her his roundabout journey from his hometown to Zakhu.

Selma told Rebwar, "My parents live across the border in Turkey and they became good friends with your brother, and Severeen. That is how we know them. Mahdy drove them back there this morning. I know Delan was hoping to connect with you somewhere. Mahdy should be back tonight," continued Selma, "So make yourself feel at home."

Rebwar told her how much he appreciated her hospitality. He went into detail how he had not seen his brother for many years.

"I got myself a permanent residency in Sweden, and a good job. I lost all my family during Saddam's chemical attack of Halabja. Everyone who knew Delan, thought he died with the rest of our family, and his body was taken by the International Red Cross to France to analyze the poison that was used. Saddam denied using chemical weapons against the Kurds, claiming it was the Iranian forces. Iran tried everything to prove that they didn't do it." Selma shook her head in sympathy.

"Are you hungry?"

Rebwar perked up at the offer. "I came into town early this morning and I have been looking for Delan all day long. I can't remember if I've even had water to drink, much less food."

Selma smiled. "I made supper. You will eat some." Rebwar at first resisted the offer and thanked her. But she insisted. "I don't think you will even find a restaurant that is open in town. The situation here is deteriorating everyday. Besides, Mahdy should be home shortly." And she disappeared into the kitchen.

Selma quickly returned into the room and whispered, "By the way, I have something for you that Delan left here. Come with me."

Rebwar got up and followed Selma to the bedroom, where she threw off a pile of blankets on top of an old chest and opened it. Rebwar was silent, perplexed.

Finally, way down in the trunk under a bunch of clean sheets and rags, her fingers came across the precious items. She handed him Delan's sketchbook.

"Shhh! Please. Just take it. " Carefully she offered him the book.

Opening its stiff pages, Rebwar's eyes widened at the drawings of sick and starving refugees in a camp.

"We need to keep this hidden," Selma whispered. "If Hussein's men show up, they would not want this evidence revealed to the world." Rebwar was speechless.

Selma turned for the kitchen, leaving him to absorb each line, each face, each page of the sketchbook.

A short while later, returning with a tray of food, she found him still sitting on the futon studying his brother's work.

"Beautiful, isn't it?" she said reverently.

Looking up from the drawings, she could see the tears in his eyes.

"I can't thank you enough. You were very brave to keep my brother's book. If you had been caught .... Thank you."

Selma and Rebwar had dinner in silence. Hours after finishing, Mahdy was still not home. Selma and Rebwar started to worry. They could hear the sporadic sound of machine gun fire around town. Suddenly, Mahdy burst through the door and when he saw Selma, hugged her, saying, "It was a really rough ride home."

"Mahdy, I want you to meet someone," said Selma, indicating their visitor. Rebwar stood up to greet him.

"Oh, my God," Mahdy said excitedly, "You must be Delan's brother, Rebwar, from Sulaymaniyah!"

They shook hands and Mahdy continued, "Delan and Severeen are staying in my father-in-law's house just across the border."

"This is great news to hear!" said Rebwar.

"Unfortunately", warned Mahdy, " we cannot travel at night. It is not safe at all. But I will take you there in the morning. You might as well make yourself comfortable and spend the night here with us."

The next day, Rebwar with his duffel bag in his hand, thanked Selma for her kind hospitality and got into the taxi with Mahdy. The road was so congested with cars and pedestrians, all heading towards the border for safety.

Snura

Meanwhile, Delan and Severeen were staying in Snura, at Ezamalden's house. Severeen sat helplessly watching Shamsa and Shanaz doing their laundry by hand. She offered to assist them. In their polite way, they refused. "Our guests are not supposed to be working in our house", said Shamsa, "Besides these are our chores."

Delan was restless, not knowing what to do about his brother, except to stay in Snura for now, and hopefully, he would connect with someone in Zakhu who might know Mahdy's whereabouts..

Ezamalden invited Delan and Severeen out to the front porch. He explained that in the last twenty years, this very small village had become the center for illegals crossing the border, and it became very vulnerable and exposed to shootouts between the Turkish military forces and the Kurdish resistant group, PKK. The silence of the night was interrupted often by the sound of assault rifles for hours. The next day is when everyone would find out who was gunned down the night before.

Now, only thirty homes remain standing. The homes are in ruins. Only the foundations and adobe walls remained, like melting candles. The military forces always assumed the villagers were connected with the PKK. For this reason, the few families that stay advise their children when they are grown to leave, like a bird leaves the nest, so they won't be killed in the crossfire between the Turkish military and the PKK. Besides, they know their children will not be able to get a decent job to survive. These families are stuck between a rock and hard places because most of them were born here and love their village and would never want to leave. They really had no where else to go, due to the strict Turkish law that prevents the Kurds from living in one small area. They were not allowed to move freely around the country.

Still the people in Snura try to carry on.

It's an early Spring and there's not much to do on the farms, so most of the men get together in a one-room mosque for a little conversation with each other. The village shepherd takes the herds of goats and sheep out to the hills and meadows for grazing. He brings them back in the evening before sundown. A month before, the men pruned the grape vines and some of the fruit trees. Luscious pears and figs are still growing. They continue to plow the areas for wheat and barley, and soon seeds will be planted.

Ezamalden sighed, "You can see the seasons come and go. We used to look forward to them. Each season had a special excitement that we enjoyed. We used to do a little hunting in between. Barbecuing rabbits, ducks and pheasants were always a pleasure. Occasionally we hunted wild boar, even though we didn't eat them, for religious reasons. But it was a challenge to hunt them! We would give them to the Armenians, who enjoyed eating them."

The men chuckled at this thought.

"Unfortunately," Ezamalden continued, "those are all good memories. Now, if you get caught with a rifle, you get killed whether you were using it for hunting or not because they think you are part of the PKK Resistance.

"I made a little coffin for my hunting rifle and buried it with all the ammunitions in my backyard. The future is bleak when you cant look forward to tomorrow. We live one day at a time."

Delan and Severeen sat very quietly after Ezamalden's remarks. After a repose, Delan stood announcing, "Severeen and I are going to take a little walk on the road towards the border. Maybe I can do some sketches while I'm there. It's a beautiful day."

"You have to be very careful, " warned Ezamalden.

With backpacks over their shoulders, the couple disappeared around the bend. They soon found themselves walking alongside a stream of melting snow, away from the main road. They were quite enchanted by the brilliant colors of the grass and flowers so they stopped to look more closely at the shiny leaves of newly sprouted shrubs and trees.

They continued walking and were excited when they came upon the narcissus. Delan picked one blade and inhaled the bouquet. He then handed it over to Severeen. Then he picked another flower for himself and inhaled it. He was intoxicated by the fragrance and taken back through time and space.

"It's amazing how the temperature drops as soon as the sun goes down and all these wildflowers resist the freeze," Delan sighed. "Some of the fragrances get very intense, like that of the narcissus When the stream dries out around May or June, the bulbs of the narcissus go dormant deep under the ground until next year. In spite of its beauty and fragrance, narcissus is really the symbol of the Spring bringing a new life forces and freedom, for it coincides with the Kurdish New Year, Newroz."

For the Kurdish people, Newroz is the most important day of the year. Over 2700 years ago the Kurds rebelled against the monarch for their liberation, which they enjoyed until 1917, when the Ottoman Empire lost World War I. The British Empire had created the kingdoms and many small Emirates in order to control their oil on the Persian and Arabian gulfs. Iraq was one of those countries created. Kurdistan was divided because the Kurds wanted to have control over their land and natural resources.

Thinking of his Kurdish past and his people's hopeful future, Delan reveled in the fantasy and closed his eyes. And when he opened them again, it was as if all his dreams were realized, as Severeen's face filled his view. Pulling her closer, the two embraced.

***

Later, as Delan passed the time thumbing through many sketchbooks in his backpack, he suddenly flashed on Zakhu, remembering the images he sketched there. Realizing that all his sketchbooks were not in his bag, he turned to Severeen in a panic, "I left one of my sketchbooks at Mahdy's house. It was the one with the drawings of the refugees and the camp."

"Don't worry. When we see Mahdy, we can tell him to bring it the next time he drives back here."

"No, Severeen, you don't understand. If those drawings are discovered by Hussein's men Mahdy and Selma could be executed! My name is on them. They will hunt me down!"

Caressing his furrowed brow, she whispered, "We have to believe they will not be found."

Severeen's words calmed him. Pulling a few loose pages from his backpack, he began a lighthearted sketch of Severeen, smiling at him. But her countenance saddened, when out of the corner of her eye she spotted, off in the distance, people hurriedly trekking down the rocky mountain.

"Delan, over there." Severeen pointed toward the people.

Delan's pencil stopped. "They are in quite a hurry. I hope everything is okay."

The couple watched the travellers until they could decipher the figures as weary men, loaded down with backpacks and gear. As they neared Delan waved. "Where are you coming from?"

After a thoughtful hesitation, one of the men approached, extending his hand. "I'm Nigel and this is Mark. We work for the British Press. We are covering the refugee camp not far from here."

Still breathing hard the tired man wanted to continue talking, but could not catch his breath. Delan took the moment to introduce himself and Severeen. But before he could complete the pleasantries, Mark spoke up.

"We'd better be going. They'll be looking for us."

"Looking for you? Who?"

"A few miles after leaving the camp we found ourselves in a crossfire. We don't know who was shooting, but we could tell it was assault rifles and mortars. All we could do was duck, run and get out of the way. In the confusion our co-worker, Emmy, went a different direction. We don't know if she's even alive."

"What are you guys doing here?" Nigel interrupted with a hint of cautious curiosity.

"I'm from Paris, and Delan my fiancé, is from Halabja, Kurdistan. We were on our way back there, but couldn't get very far due to the uprising. So, we came back here in the hopes of finding Delan's brother. We are staying with friends in the village of Snura, just a few miles from here."

The foursome soon agreed to travel back to Snura together.

But as Severeen and Delan packed their backpacks, two military jeeps crossed the bridge, headed for them. Before the quartet knew could move the soldiers, with rifles raised, surrounded Delan, Severeen and the journalists.

As the travellers stood petrified, an officer jumped out of the jeep and walked over to them. "We spotted you two running down the other side of the mountain."

After a nervous pause Nigel broke the silence. "Sir, we work for the British press," he gestured to Mark. "There was a lot of shooting back there and we were simply trying to getting out of the way. In the process we lost track of our co-worker. In the confusion we don't know which way she went."

The officer studied the Westerners for a tense moment, then requested their passports; which the journalists instantly handed over.

As the officer examined the paperwork and their journalist identification cards, he mused, "How do we know you are not with the terrorists? We were chasing them and saw you two running the same way."

"You can take us back to the refugee camps." Mark offered. "They will tell you that we have been there for three days."

The officer waved to his car. A moment later a Kurdish man was escorted out of the vehicle at gunpoint. "This terrorist claims you two are with the terrorists."

Approaching his Kurdish prisoner, the officer pointed to the journalists, "Did you see these two running away from the scene?"

The Kurd, looking down at the ground mumbled, "Yes, sir."

Turning to the journalists the soldier calmly observed, "You must have been covering the terrorist PKK, and not the refugee camps. Otherwise, why were you in that crossfire?"

Nigel and Mark stood speechless.

The officer ordered the soldiers to search the two men, which they did very roughly. They took their cameras and smashed them. The poor journalists pleaded for help, claiming they had nothing to do with the terrorists. The officer didn't believe them and commanded the soldiers to beat them.

The officer then turned to Delan and Severeen. "Who are you, and what are you doing here?" Not waiting for their answers, he asked for their IDs. They turned them over to the officer, as both alternately gave him different parts of their story.

"How did you get a French passport?" Not giving Delan a chance to answer, he motioned to his superior.

A high ranking officer sauntered over to the frightened couple, and studied Delan, "I remember you..."

A vague familiar flash registered in the artist's eyes; the soldier was at the Turkish security checkpoint when they crossed over the border.

"Isn't your homeland south of here?"

"Yes," Delan answered with friendly smile, "We are trying to get back to our family."

"So you say." He stepped closer. "Yet here you are. What's keeping you? Are you delayed Stuck?"

"Yes, for a long time. It seems that we are ALL stuck... between Iraq" Delan glances at the blood splattered faces of the journalists, then back at the familiar officer, "and hard places."

The officer stepped back, with a chuckle.

"Between Iraq and hard places. You are a clever, Kurd." His smile faded. "But then spies have to be. Are you working for the French government? Maybe you are here to join the rebels? Kurds! You are all troublemakers!"

With a stern wave of his hand he signaled his soldiers, and immediately the couple's backpacks were ripped open. It wasn't long before the artist's sketchbook fell to the ground, casting Delan's pearls before the swine. But to them the illustrations were not even contraband; just a few landscapes and portraits of Severeen and Ezamalden's son.

The soldiers kept beating the journalists until they were on the ground bleeding. The officer separated Severeen from Delan and commanded that the soldiers beat Delan, as well.

Still rifling through their belongings the soldiers found no weapons or cameras, only the Red Cross emblem in Severeen's backpack.

Peering at Severeen with his steely brown-black eyes, the commander held up the insignia, "You work with the Red Cross?" "Yes, sir."

"You help patients whether they are civilians – or rebels? Even the PKK?

"Sir, I volunteer at a refugee camp on the Iraqi side. They are all waiting for the border to open so they can cross over to Turkey."

By now the two journalists were in bad shape, moaning helplessly on the ground. Delan, too was moaning, begging them to stop, which prompted the soldiers to beat him with more gusto.

Severeen could not take much more. Finally all the pain, blood, frustration and injustice she had witnessed rose within her, and with Delan's screams of pain in her ears she let go, like an uncorked volcano. "Please, sir, my fiancé was a victim of the poison gas in Halabja and was taken to a French hospital for treatment without any of his Kurdish identification, so the French government provided him with his papers. That's where we met. I was a nurse in that hospital. Since then we have been trying to get back to Delan's hometown to see if any of his family survived. That is why we are here, in Snura."

The officer laughed, "You expect us to believe you?"

"We can go and verify all this information on the other side of the border if you wish."

Irritated by her defiant air, the officer commanded that Severeen be restrained, and that Delan be beat again this time with the butts of their rifles.

As they pummeled the artist, they cursed him yelling, "Kurdish troublemaker!" "Terrorist!" And over their slander, Severeen continually begged them to "Stop!!" For this, she, too was struck. Falling to the ground, bleeding, next to Delan.

The officer, now heady with power, ordered the soldiers to bring the Kurdish man a pistol. And in a cold, steady voice he commanded, "Shoot these two terrorists now."

The man started to cry, "Please, sir, I am just a farmer. I have never harmed anyone and I don't know these two men. Please let me go."

"If you want to save your own life, then you will do as ordered!"

The soldiers holding the trembling farmer put their guns to his head, and were about to shoot, when the farmer called to the journalists, in tears, "Please forgive me." He pulled the trigger twice, and the journalists felt no more pain.

The officer came back to Severeen and said, "You saw it. You are witness. The Kurdish terrorist shot those two men."

Severeen shut her eyes and cried.

The officer walked away, looked at his soldiers, and giving them an approving nod, they coldly shot the Kurdish farmer in the head.

As the lifeless body fell to the ground, the soldiers walked away, giving Delan, another kick to the head, as they passed.

As soldiers' jeeps disappeared, Severeen lifted her bloody frame from the ground. Though injured, she forced herself to reach her fiancé. Checking Delan's head wounds and vital signs, she summoned all of her strength and skill to stop the bleeding. Frantically she searched her backpack for cloth and salve to clean and wrap his battered head. But the bleeding could not be stopped.

"Why!?" she cried out in helpless frustration, "Why must they massacre the innocent?"

The sound of her voice aroused Mark, prompting the wounded journalist to move and groan, catching Severeen's attention.

Propping Delan's head and shoulders up against his backpack, she whispered, "I will get you help, my love." Delan smiled weakly.

Moving to the fallen journalists, the nurse was surprised to find Mark still alive. Motioning her closer, he attempted with great difficulty to communicate.

"Please," he whispered with his last breath, "Here." Pointing to the lower part of his jacket, his arm fell limp. He was gone.

In a state of shock she began to dig through the many pockets of his jacket, finding nothing. Desperately she turned his body on its side, and there she spotted another pocket inside the jacket.

Plunging her hand into its depths she retrieved a fist full of film. Digging her hand in again, she discovered even more rolls.

Securing the evidence in a compartment of her backpack, she returned to Delan. Leaning against her bag, she lovingly placed his head in her lap and tried to catch her breath.

For a long while she waited, hoping, fearing that someone would come.

Just as daylight faded and she started to doze, bright headlights flashed across her face. It was a car coming towards them from the other side of the bridge. It looked like... yes, Mahdy's white taxi!

Waiving excitedly Severeen whispered to Delan, "Hold on, my love!"

Spotting Severeen's signal in the half-light, the car skidded to a stop. And Mahdy rushed across the bridge, slowing only to take in the carnage around him.

"Oh, my God! What happened here?" As he paused, Rebwar ran past him, falling to his knees next to his bleeding brother. "Oh, my sweet Delan, are you -?"

Recognizing the familiar voice Delan forced his eyes open.

"It's so good to see you, too, Rebwar."

Taking Delan's hand the two brothers were united again

"My sister... my little nephews?"

"They are all fine. Please, don't talk."

"Last time I was with the family and friends," Delan struggled to continue, "they were all dead. I kept hoping it was a nightmare." Subconsciously, the artist knew the little daylight they had left would soon be gone, and pressed on, "When are they going to stop killing us? Life is so beautiful, so precious. But my family is here, with me…"

Gripping his brother's hand with all his waning strength, Delan turned his gaze to Severeen, "My family is here… Severeen, I love you."

Though his breathing grew heavy, and his eyes communicated intense pain, he kept his focus on his beloved Severeen. Soon, a single tear fell to his cheek, reflecting the sunset's last light. Still, Delan refused to close his eyes. He wanted the last image painted on the canvas of his soul to be the ultimate portrait, Severeen's smile.

***

Six months later…

On a little Paris side street, just off the Rue Vielle du temple, a new gallery opened its doors for a unique exhibit. Winding down the cobblestone street, a meandering mix of socialites, activists, art critics and average folk waited for their turn inside the converted warehouse;. It seemed everyone was drawn to the controversial collection.

Inside the white-walled exhibit, Severeen sipped wine, engrossed in pleasant conversation. Then out of the corner of her eyes, she noticed two familiar faces amid the crowd.

"Almas! Ronak! You're here!"

Excusing herself she navigated her way through the press of art enthusiasts and rushed to embrace the newlyweds.

"I am so glad you two came." "How could we not?" Almas' voice broke with emotion. "He was an artist, our friend."

"What you have accomplished here is amazing," Ronak beamed gesturing to the menagerie of spot lit displays. "Its... inspiring."

Surrounding the trio of old friends was a montage of mayhem. On every wall hung sacred, silent scenes that spoke far louder than any propaganda. Displayed were all the photographs Severeen salvaged from the pockets of the fallen journalists, Mark and Nigel. Each frame was a visual witness to the destruction and death that always comes with war. Each image snapped was an indictment against every heartless dictator.

Mixed in, among the photographs, were the contrasting sketches and paintings of Delan; his pencil renderings of Severeen's many moods, the life-affirming images of Ezamalden's playful boy, the colorful-canvased landscapes of snow-covered mountains and waving fields of narcissus.

But among Delan's many displays of fantasy, Severeen also included his haunting reminder of every Kurd's reality; the crumbling buildings of a once bustling village, and a living mother cradling her dead child.

"...And this is Delan's most important work," Severeen directed her friends to a small canvas, resting on an old grass stained easel. "It's the one painting he never got around to finishing, but its message is one every generation should heed."

"That sounds foreboding," Almas smiled, studying the canvas closely. "It's just a beautiful painting of three horse playing in a field."

"Don't be deceived by the beauty," Severeen warned, "Delan said that the animals were not playful, but agitated... for they sensed what was coming."

~

About the Author

Zuhdi Sardar was born and raised in Sulaymaniyah, Kurdistan (Iraq). There, he grew to see the world through artistic eyes, and went on to develop his talents at the Fine Arts Institute of Baghdad.

Coming to America in 1964, Zuhdi used his new-found freedom to further explore his passion for painting. That zeal, fueled by his concern for his war-torn homeland, ultimately earned Sardar a grant to study at the prestigious Academy of Art in Paris.

As a testament to his skill at illustrating the Kurdish plight on canvas, the artist's first solo collection was showcased by the American Friends of the Middle East, located in Baghdad. And building on that momentum, his second, even more compelling collection was debuted at the France-Amerique Gallery, in Paris.

Eventually becoming a top scenic artist, Zuhdi's work is not only seen in the backgrounds and props of countless Hollywood productions, but his artful remembrances of Kurdistan can be also viewed on the walls of galleries and museums throughout Southern California.

Today, Zuhdi Sardar and his wife Judith reside in Ventura County, just a stone's throw from the Los Angeles entertainment industry where he continues to thrive – not only painting imagery that speaks volumes, but also writing books that paint unforgettable pictures.

~

CPSIA information can be obtained at www.ICGtesting.com
Printed in the USA
LVOW041132041212